FUTURE fake HUSBAND

KATE HAWTHORNE
E.M. DENNING

Future Fake Husband
Kate Hawthorne & E.M. Denning

Copyright © 2018 Kate Hawthorne, E.M. Denning
Edited by: Jordan Buchanan
Cover Design: AmaiDesigns

All rights reserved. No part of this story may be used, reproduced, or transmitted in any form or by any means without the written permission of the copyright holder, except in the case of brief quotations embodied within critical reviews and articles.

This is a work of fiction. The names, characters, and incidents are products of the writer's imagination or have been used fictitiously and are not meant to be construed as real. Any resemblance to actual events, locales, persons, or organizations is entirely coincidental.

This book contains sexually explicit content which is only suitable for mature readers.

Dedication

To those who find love in unexpected places.

Chapter One
COLE

❧

"You've got to listen to reason, darling."

Cole dropped his head against the cold leather of one of his father's wingback chairs and sighed, doing his best to mentally shut out the drone of his mother's voice. She'd called him home to harass him again, about his perceived chronic bachelorhood as far as he could tell, and he wasn't interested in what she had to say.

"I do *date*, Mother," Cole grumbled.

The truth of his relationship situation lay somewhere between what his mother accused him of and what he said. Cole did date, frequently, but rarely more than a handful of times with the same person. It wasn't that he wanted to go through relationships the way he did; it was just that no one had ever held his attention.

Cole did most of his partner searching when he least intended—at lunch with his sister, at the grocery store, while chatting up a customer. He didn't enjoy the bar and club scene. His best friend, Ryan, had long given up on trying to talk him out of the house and agreed to spend time at Cole's villa at the Vineyard if he wanted to hang out on the weekends.

Cole's family owned a decent-sized and comfortably successful vineyard in the heart of California wine country. It had been in his family for generations and he'd taken over the day-to-day operations after he graduated from college. It had always been a given that he would inherit Mallory Vineyard and he'd spent his adult life preparing for it.

Not to say he wanted his parents to die, quite the opposite. His parents had little interest in maintaining the vineyard, but appreciated the family heritage of the place. His mother, Constance, had worked out a deal with her parents, the current owners, and arranged for it to pass to Cole instead of to her. Everyone had been in agreement for years.

"They're going to leave the vineyard to Kristen!" his mother shouted, a rare breach of decorum that drew his attention.

"I'm sorry, what?" Cole asked, confident he'd misheard.

"If you don't settle down, they're going to will the vineyard to Kristen." His mother collapsed into a chair opposite him.

"She doesn't even want the vineyard. She's getting married in a week and moving to Connecticut," Cole reminded her of the facts she already knew.

"Kristen will probably sell it," Constance agreed.

He raised his eyebrows at her. "Then just have them leave it to you, and you can will it to me."

"That won't happen," she lamented. "You know how your Nan gets when she gets an idea, and she's got an idea."

Cole closed his eyes and rubbed at his temples, frustrated with this unexpected turn of events.

"Does Nan know I'm gay?" he asked, opening his eyes and giving his mother a sardonic glare.

"Surprisingly, Cole, she could care less *who* you settle down with as long as you just settle down. She reminded me no less than eight times that Mallory Vineyard is a family business with a family name."

"And she'd rather let Kristen sell it off than let a bachelor take rights to it?" Cole pushed out of the chair and paced across the room to the window, resting his hands on the ledge and staring outside. His father's office had one of the best views the main house had to offer and, much to Cole's delight, it didn't face his own house that sat across the property.

"Family, Cole," his mother reminded him gently.

"This is fucking ridiculous," he muttered, slicking a hand through his short black hair. He walked back to the table he'd been sitting beside and leaned down, dropping a perfunctory kiss on his mother's cheek.

"Please be reasonable," she pleaded.

"I need a drink, Mom."

Cole left her in the study, choosing to walk the half mile across the property to his residence. He pushed the front door open then closed it tightly behind him and locked it, as if that would keep the conversation and the black cloud that had followed it out of his private space.

In his kitchen, he poured himself a glass of Cabernet and pulled his phone out of his pocket, scrolling through the hundreds of names he had stored in it.

Ginger from Starbucks.

Tattoos at Gas Station.

Kristen's baker.

Blondie at Target.

Jackson.

Caleb.

Ryan.

Cole groaned and dialed Ryan's number. He didn't answer, and Cole didn't leave a message, opting instead to finish his wine and slide his phone onto the kitchen counter. He stalked upstairs to his bedroom and kicked his shoes into his closet before stripping out of his slacks and long-sleeve button-up. He discarded his briefs, tossing everything into his hamper. He walked naked to the bathroom tucked into a corner of the bedroom and opened the glass shower door, turning the hot water on.

He stepped into the spray and squirted some soap into his hand, jerking himself off quickly—because what was the point of a shower if you didn't come—then washed himself before rinsing and stepping out to dry off.

Cole pulled a pair of clean jeans out of his dresser and a fresh pair of briefs, dressing without much thought. He ran a hand through the fuzz of his happy trail, making sure his chest and stomach were dry before he pulled on a plain black t-shirt.

Back in the kitchen, he noticed Ryan hadn't called him back, but he had two missed calls from his mom. He wasn't interested in dealing with her, so he powered off his phone and left it behind as he picked up his keys and wallet and headed out the front door.

Cole hopped into the driver's seat of his Range Rover and drove himself out of Mallory Vineyard, away from his family and these unexpected complications. He cruised through town, grumbling to himself about his grandparents the entire way. Cole had always planned on settling down and getting married, maybe even having a dog, or kids, but he was only twenty-eight. Why the rush?

He pulled into the parking lot of Tubby's and cut the engine. He went in the back door, taking a seat at the corner of the bar.

"Didn't expect to see you here tonight. Or ever."

Cole looked up and narrowed his eyes at Ivan, the bartender.

"I can leave," Cole offered, pointing toward the door he'd just entered through.

"Sure, go," Ivan said, his face unamused.

They stared at each other in silence until Cole saw the corner of Ivan's lip twitch, giving him away. His mouth split into a smile and he laughed, extending a hand across the bar to shake Cole's hand.

"Where the fuck have you been, man?" Ivan asked, pouring Cole a pint of beer. "I haven't seen you in forever. Not since you and Caleb split."

Cole's mood soured briefly, thinking about Caleb for the second time that night, which as far as he was concerned was two too many. He hadn't thought much about Caleb in the past year and he liked it that way. Even if he'd been with Caleb when this ultimatum from his Nan had come down, he wouldn't have married him.

Thankfully, Caleb had broken up with him before Cole had been forced to make that call.

"I've just been running Mallory," he answered, taking a drink of his beer.

"Is it yours yet?"

Cole shook his head.

"What about you? What have you been up to?" he asked, hoping to change the subject.

"Oh, you know. Just glad it's tourist season." Ivan grinned a bit mischievously.

Cole rolled his eyes; his old friend from high school had quite a reputation for being a ladies' man. With wavy brown hair and bright blue eyes, Ivan hadn't ever had an issue talking his way into the beds of the myriad of bridesmaids, sorority girls, and middle-aged divorcees that rolled through town in the summer.

"How many this year?" Cole asked, taking another long pull of his drink.

"A gentleman doesn't kiss and tell," Ivan said, feigning horror. "Definitely not six."

Cole laughed and shook his head.

A group of people from the other end of the bar called Ivan away, but he poured Cole a fresh pint before disappearing. Cole finished his first drink and started on his second, thinking back to the earlier conversation with his mom.

The thought that his Nan would leave Kristen the vineyard just because he wasn't in a long-term and legally-binding relationship was beyond frustrating. Kristen was twenty-three and vapid, focused solely on the number of zeroes in her fiancé Edward's bank account.

It was six zeroes; Cole knew because his father had told him. Like Cole had any concern about money or how much Kristen would have to play with once she suckered poor Edward Fulton into marrying her on the white sand beaches of French Polynesia.

As much as Cole wasn't interested in watching Edward ruin his life by tying himself to Kristen, he was looking forward to five days and four nights on a private strip of beach. He didn't have a date and briefly debated if finding a date worthy of a family wedding would possibly be enough to convince his Nan that Mallory should be left to him like they'd always planned.

Half a pint later, he decided it was a half-baked idea.

A sharp bark of laughter at the other end of the bar drew his attention. Leaning forward, he looked toward the sound in time to watch Ivan angle himself toward a busty blonde who was laughing in that painfully obvious, pay-attention-to-me kind of way.

He could get involved with a woman, he thought. It would be a total facade, but could potentially appease his family if they acted convincingly enough. They'd have to reach an agreement, of course, since Cole wasn't attracted to women, but if they could each have their own dalliances on the side...

Another half a pint later, he decided that was an even worse idea than the first one.

Cole sighed, without a clue as to what he should do.

Chapter Two
RHETT

※

"I swear, you seem so normal, and then I call you and you're playing the same song on repeat in the background. And it's not even a good song."

"If you're going to insult my favorite band, I have no problem hanging up on you," Rhett responded to his older-by-three-minutes brother, Ryan. "What do you want? I'm busy."

Ryan laughed so loud Rhett had to pull the phone away from his ear. "You are not busy. You're listening to some sort of folk-rock hybrid, whatever, while you doodle table settings and lighting ideas in your sketchbook."

"Hanging up now," Rhett said as he pulled the phone away from his ear again.

"Fine, fine. I'll get to the point. I ran into Neil today."

Rhett rolled his eyes. "And how is Neil?" Overcome with the urge to stab his pen through the pages of his sketchbook, Rhett closed it and set it safely aside. He removed his glasses and rubbed at his eyes before putting them back on.

"He says he misses you."

Rhett stood up and balled his fist. "If you gave him my number, I'm going to key your car, Ryan. I promise I will."

"I thought you'd be happy to hear he missed you. You were a wreck when you broke up."

Rhett exhaled an ugly laugh. "We didn't break up. He dumped me. In public. I'm not an emotional masochist so it's not something I care to repeat."

"Well, then it's a good thing I didn't give him your number. You really ought to start dating again though. It's not like you to be single for so long."

It really wasn't, but after the very public humiliation of his last breakup, Rhett decided he'd be better off not being in a relationship for a while. He missed the comfort of it, but it was something he learned he could live without.

He loved getting to know someone new, learning their likes and dislikes, the little physical tics they had, their bad habits. He liked the feeling a new relationship gave him, that glimmer of hope that maybe, *maybe*, this was the one.

"I'm fine on my own, Ryan. Single isn't so bad; besides, I have Lucy."

Ryan groaned. "A fern is not a pet, Rhett. You can't talk to a houseplant and tell me that it's a proper substitute for human interaction."

"Are you sure about that? I've met some of your exes. They don't exactly pass for human either."

"Touché, baby brother." Ryan exhaled. "Look, normally I really couldn't care less who you may or may not be dating, but Dad asked me to ask you."

Their dad had done the best he could to raise them on his own after their mother died when they were in the eighth grade. He owned his own company, and it continued to make a nice profit over the years. Rhett and Ryan had never wanted for much, but when it came to the emotional things, like worrying about your kid's happiness, their dad had always had a hard time talking to them. He'd said it was because he wasn't very close with his parents, so he wasn't sure how to talk about certain things. He'd said their mother had always handled that. And now, with her gone, it was his method to approach one boy when he was concerned about the other. He found it easier to just relay his concerns and hope they sorted out the issue between the two of them with no further need of his input.

Rhett sighed; there was only one possible way to get Ryan off his back and stop their dad from worrying. He had to lie.

"Look, I didn't want to say anything, but I've been seeing someone. It's new, but I really like him and I don't want to jinx it, okay? Happy now?" He hated lying and tried to never do it, but that meant when he finally did lie to someone, they were more apt to buy into his bullshit. Like Ryan did—hook, line, and sinker.

"You little shit. Who are you seeing? You have to tell me. I know just about everyone in town."

"I'm not telling, Ryan. I like him, a lot. He's good to me. He's...nice."

"Nice? That's the best you can give me? Is he hot? Does he give good head?"

"I'm not telling you that." Rhett wrinkled his nose. In his head, his imaginary boyfriend was absolutely hot. He refused to think of anything more than that while still on the phone with his brother.

"Fine, be like that. Look, I have to go, but I'll call you later and harass you for more details about your mystery man."

"Talk soon," Rhett said as he ended the call. He looked at Lucy, the potted fern that sat on his table. "Don't look at me like that. I had to tell him something. He's relentless. Three minutes older and he thinks that somehow makes me less capable of running my life than he is."

Rhett walked past Lucy, and headed for his bedroom. He slipped into a pair of clean jeans and a long-sleeved burgundy t-shirt that he'd stolen from one of his exes because it looked better on him.

Walking past Lucy again, he nodded to the plant. "Don't wait up," he said as he walked out the door.

Usually he'd stay home and marathon one of his favorite television shows, but his conversation with Ryan had left him unsettled and in need of a distraction. And if he was willing to admit that Ryan was right—which he wasn't—a potted plant really wasn't a good substitute for human interaction.

Living a few blocks from downtown, Rhett left his car in its spot and walked to Tubby's. Being tourist season, it was busy as hell, but Rhett managed to get a glass of something on tap before finding an empty seat at the far end of the bar.

He drank half his beer, then stared at the other half, suddenly unsure why he'd come out to begin with. He wasn't in the mood to chat up a random stranger. His best friend, Penny, was at home with her husband and their baby, and she'd murder him in his sleep if he called and woke Tyson. He was just about to go home and be content with the fact that he'd at least had different scenery to be miserable in for a while, when someone sat down next to him.

"Hey, Rhett. Long time, no see."

Rhett turned his head and came face to face with Cole Mallory and his gorgeous sage green eyes. Not only was he the heir to the Mallory Vineyard, but he was a walking wet dream and his brother's best friend.

"You saw me last week. I was at the Vineyard with Macy for the Carlson-Schmidt wedding."

Cole leaned closer, his cologne light and rich, enticing and slightly spicy. "I meant outside of work. In a place like this." Cole took a sip of his drink and eyed Rhett. "What are you doing here anyway?"

"My brother is a pain in the ass."

Cole's eyebrows shot up, then he nodded. "A pain in the ass who doesn't answer his phone."

Rhett rolled his eyes. "He was probably talking to me. Dad is worried because I'm single."

Cole's laughter surprised him and Rhett stared at him until he was done.

"You and I have more in common than I thought."

"Is your family on your ass, too?"

Cole stood up and motioned to the back corner where a booth had just become available. Rhett grabbed his drink and followed, taking the seat opposite him.

"Is there some sort of rule parents have that says their kids need to be settled down by the time they're twenty-five?" Cole began to rant. "I wasn't aware that I was the male equivalent of a spinster. In a brand new twist of fuckery, I have to get married or the vineyard will go to my idiot sister, who probably only cares how many vacations she could fund with the proceeds of its sale."

"Spinsters were unmarried, but they were also virgins. You haven't been a virgin since the ninth grade."

"Your brother has a big mouth," Cole said, taking a swig of his beer.

Rhett grimaced. "Please don't talk about my brother like that. I don't need the details."

Cole choked, covering his mouth as he coughed and hacked until his face turned slightly red. He managed to not do a spit-take all over the table, but only barely.

"Your brother and I are close, but not that close."

"Too bad, or you could marry him and shut your family up. He'd do it just to get to drive that fancy car of yours."

"No one would believe it. They know Ryan and me too well. We love each other, but we'd kill each other. It wouldn't be believable. My spouse would have to be someone they'd be able to see me with." Cole looked at Rhett, raking his gaze over him as if he were examining him.

"What?" Rhett patted his cheeks, feeling suddenly self-conscious. He'd never had Cole Mallory pay such close attention to him before. Rhett had always been the non-entity in the background. Not exactly ignored, Cole wasn't rude like that, but he was Ryan's friend and Rhett and Ryan had always run with different crowds. "What?" he asked again when Cole's smile grew.

"It's not a bad idea. At first, I thought I was nuts for even considering something like it, but I think it could work."

"What?" Rhett was beginning to feel a little like a parrot and he drank the rest of his beer as Cole's smile brightened.

"I could marry you."

Chapter Three
COLE

"I'm sorry, what?" Rhett stammered, spitting his beer onto the table. He quickly reached between them and used his hand to wipe it up then rubbed his hand on his pants.

"I could marry you," Cole repeated, the idea forming more fully in his head the longer he thought about it.

Marrying Rhett was totally feasible *and* something he could easily convince his family was legit. Rhett's brother was his best friend. He'd known them both his entire life; it was completely possible that he'd fallen for his best friend's bookish twin brother.

"I can pay you or something, if you want, to go along with it," Cole continued excitedly.

"Pay me?" Rhett asked, looking slightly horrified. "Am I a prostitute? We've moved from spinsters to escorts?"

"The proper term is sex worker, Rhett, and no, I'm not offering to pay you for sex. I'm offering to pay you to pretend to be my husband." Cole had already made up his mind this idea was brilliant. This was his chance to save his future.

"How would we explain to Ryan that we're suddenly engaged?" Rhett questioned.

"Well, we wouldn't get engaged right away, but we could tell people we'd been seeing each other in secret or something. We wanted to keep things just between us for as long as we could."

Something Cole couldn't identify flashed across Rhett's face and his cheeks turned pink.

"What?" Cole asked. "Why are you blushing?"

Rhett's hands flew to his cheeks and covered them, eyes wide and head shaking side to side.

"Tell me," Cole pressed, leaning over the table closer to Rhett.

He inhaled sharply and pulled back, confused. Had Rhett always smelled this good? Like clean sheets and fruit, the smell resonated with Cole, imprinting a fantasy in his head of Rhett wrapped in luxurious cotton sheets, eating strawberries and drinking wine.

Cole shook his head to clear it, unsure of where a thought like that had materialized from. He'd known Ryan and Rhett since they were kids. He'd always been closer with Ryan, the more outgoing of the twins. Rhett was always around, though, with his wire-rimmed glasses and his nose in a book of some kind, not quite as classically good looking as Ryan, but nothing you'd want to shake a stick at. He'd just been different. Ryan and Cole played tennis and took swimming, while Rhett was in AP Physics and math club.

He'd never looked at Ryan as more than a friend, and he'd definitely never looked at Rhett as more than that either, but suddenly he couldn't shake the new picture in his head that Rhett's scent evoked.

"I lied to him," Rhett whispered, dropping his hands into his lap. "I told him tonight that I was seeing someone so he'd leave me alone about it."

Cole grinned and clapped his hands. "This is perfect, Rhett! He already thinks you're seeing someone and, if you didn't tell him who, we can just let him know it's me."

"You need to slow down, Cole," Rhett said, holding his hands up between them.

Cole suddenly liked the way Rhett said his name and liked the fact that he talked with his hands. He finished off his beer in an attempt to drown his new fascination.

"Even if we convince people we're in a relationship, that's one thing. But you're talking about getting married." Rhett lifted his glasses and rubbed the bridge of his nose.

"People get divorced all the time. Like fifty percent of people," Cole offered.

"How long would we have to be fake married for?"

"Until my Nan dies, probably. She's the one saying I need to be settled down." Cole clenched his jaw, upset all over again at the ridiculous and frankly medieval insistence that he legally bind himself to another person to inherit what should by all rights be his. He was the one who ran the vineyard; he was the one that had put in the hours and the work. More than his parents and definitely more than his sister.

"And when is that going to be? Although to be honest with you, I feel like a giant creep having this conversation." Rhett winced.

"It is gritty," Cole agreed. "We should have another drink."

He grabbed their empty glasses and jumped out of the booth, practically skipping to the bar. He ordered two fresh pints and dropped them back on the table, finding Rhett's face wearing the same pained expression as when he got up.

"A few years," Cole finally answered, taking a long pull of his beer.

"So you expect me to just be celibate the entire time we're fake married?" Rhett asked, that brilliant blush from before creeping down his throat. Cole hadn't ever seen someone blush in reverse before, but somehow with Rhett, it made sense.

"You could fuck other people," Cole advised him, even though the thought of Rhett fucking anybody frankly made him rage with jealousy.

Where the fuck did that come from?

"They just couldn't tell," he added.

Rhett exhaled and took a small drink of his beer, then a larger one, and an even larger one.

"And what about you?" Rhett asked him, shoving a lock of chocolate brown hair out of his face. "You've been sleeping your way through the valley for years now. You're just going to give that up? Because there's no way the amount of men you go through is going to be able to keep quiet about your extra-marital affairs."

Cole winced, scratching at the side of his forehead to hide the look on his face.

"Is that what you think I do?" he asked, hoping he masked at least a small portion of his hurt at Rhett's insinuation.

"Is it not?" Rhett retorted, eyebrows raised in symmetrical arches over the frame of his glasses. His golden brown eyes held oceans of curiosity.

Fuck. Had he ever looked into Rhett's eyes before today?

Cole chewed his lip between his teeth, unsure of how truthful to be with Rhett before he reasoned he needed to be completely transparent if he was serious about trying to make him his fake husband.

"I don't sleep with all of them," he admitted. "And it's not like I'm a slut or anything. Even if I *had* fucked them all, it wouldn't make me a slut, but I just didn't get along with them. Like, it's fine for a bit, but when I get to know them I can just tell it won't work so what's the point of dragging it out?"

Cole swallowed and rubbed his palms down the condensation on his pint glass. Rhett didn't say anything for a long while and Cole hoped he hadn't overstepped, but he found himself surprisingly unable to look up and check.

They sat in the booth, the silence growing between them. Cole drank his entire beer, and Rhett still hadn't spoken. He dared a glance up and found Rhett's stare focused on a blank spot on the table.

"Rhett?"

Rhett looked up, blinking, like he hadn't realized how long they'd been sitting there in what was quickly becoming an increasingly uncomfortable silence.

"I don't want your money," Rhett finally spoke, "necessarily."

"What does that mean?" Cole asked, hopeful this meant Rhett was considering the proposal for the fake proposal.

"I want to have my own business," Rhett told him, drawing a shape on the table with a long finger.

"Okay..." Cole said, leading him to continue.

"I want to be an event planner."

"Isn't that what you do? Like, your family already anyway?" Cole asked, confused.

"No. My dad owns a rental company so we rent out all the stuff people need for events, but don't really do the planning. I want to do the planning," Rhett corrected him.

"Oh."

"I don't have the resources to get that off the ground though."

"Alright," Cole said, still not following.

"You do."

Oh.

There it was.

"You want my connections?" Cole questioned, tipping his head to the side and assessing Rhett, who had apparently picked up negotiating skills in one of those books he'd spent so much time in when they were kids.

"I want your help," Rhett told him.

"How can I help? I mean, I can give you money," Cole started, but Rhett silenced him by waving a hand between them.

"Not everything is about money, Cole," he hissed sharply.

"You need money to start a business, Rhett. Everyone knows that."

"I *have* money," Rhett informed him. "I'll probably need a little more capital, but I've been saving. I need help with marketing and stuff like that. Connections to people who *need* events planned. Like, if you could drop my name around the vineyard, that's what I need. Things like that."

"So you're saying I help you get your business started and you'll pretend to marry me?" Cole couldn't believe the solution was this simple. He'd get the vineyard and he'd get to have more fantasies about Rhett? What could be better than that?

"I can plan our wedding," Rhett whispered, his eyes scanning around the table like he was building a blueprint or something. "I can plan our wedding!" he repeated, looking up and grinning so broadly at Cole that it made his chest tight.

Cole's hope tripped up inside of him.

"Speaking of weddings," he said, scratching the back of his head. "This might kind of be a crash course in being my boyfriend."

"What?" Rhett asked him with a twisted look on his face.

"Kristen is getting married next weekend in Tahiti," Cole told him, fully aware that Rhett had to know about it because there wasn't anyone in the valley that *didn't* know about it.

"I know," Rhett snarked at him, clearly not understanding the implication.

"So, if I have a boyfriend that is so serious I'm going to be proposing to him in the near future, he'll probably need to come to the wedding with me."

Rhett's face paled and he leaned back in the booth, thumping his head against the black vinyl with a thud.

"Tahiti?"

"Five days. Four nights," Cole confirmed.

"Well," Rhett said after a minute had passed. "I'm overdue for a vacation."

Cole's jaw dropped.

"Are you serious?" he asked. "You'll do it?"

Rhett scrunched his face together and shrugged his shoulders. "I guess, yeah. I mean it's not like I have much else going for me."

"Rhett, you're a literal lifesaver!" Cole jumped up from his seat and slid into the booth beside Rhett, wrapping him in a hug, trying to not smell him again.

"Well, you're an actual business starter," Rhett exhaled into Cole's embrace.

"What's going on here?"

A familiar voice from behind Cole turned him and Rhett both to stone. Cole listened to Rhett's harsh breaths as they fell against his ear before he turned and looked over his shoulder at Ryan standing a few feet away with his arms crossed over his chest. Not only was he taller than Rhett, but he was broader, and blonder, and his brown eyes stared down at them with ferocious curiosity.

"Uhm, well," Rhett stammered before Cole could find words. "I guess I should introduce you to my boyfriend."

Chapter Four

RHETT

Rhett forced himself to stay close to Cole's side; it wasn't a hardship of any sort actually. Being hugged by Cole, being the source of his happiness, had felt oddly good and satisfying all at once. He wished he'd had more than three nanoseconds to enjoy it before Ryan burst into their bubble. He knew Ryan would have questions and he hoped for both his and Cole's sakes that he didn't pry too deep before they got a chance to get their story straight.

"Boyfriend?" Ryan's expression went from confusion to incredulity and his gaze snapped back and forth between them. "I don't believe you."

To his shock, Cole kissed Rhett's cheek and hugged him tighter. "Believe it."

Ryan helped himself to the seat that Cole had been occupying a minute ago and eyed them skeptically. "The serial dater with Mr. Monogamy?"

"It's why we didn't want to say anything," Rhett piped up, putting his hand tentatively on Cole's knee, surprised by how easy he found it to touch Cole. He'd never touched him before, not that he could remember. He felt bad for the way he'd made Cole feel earlier. He hadn't meant to imply that he was a slut, but he'd been on more dates than anyone Rhett knew. His explanation made sense to Rhett, though, and had him wondering how much time he'd wasted with the wrong people himself.

Rhett took a sip of his drink and looked at Ryan. "We weren't sure it would get past the first few dates, so we kept it quiet. The chemistry is there, obviously, but we wanted to be sure before we said anything."

"When were you planning on saying something?"

"Soon, actually. I've asked Rhett to come to Tahiti with me for Kristen's wedding. Not to steal the princess's thunder, but I was going to formally introduce Rhett as my boyfriend before we left."

Ryan leaned back, watching them both, and Rhett couldn't help the fear that sliced through him. If Ryan found out it was all a sham, a ruse, a mutually beneficial arrangement, he'd be pissed at Rhett for using Cole the way he was.

Cole's fingers tightened on Rhett's shoulder and he took a deep breath.

"This is really weird," Ryan said, leaning forward. "How did this even happen?"

Cole shrugged a shoulder. "I got stood up one night and I happened to run into Rhett. He did me a favor and had dinner with me so I wouldn't feel like a complete tool, and we had a lot of fun. I asked if we could do it again sometime and it progressed from there."

Rhett hung on to Cole's every word, committing them to memory as if there would be a quiz later.

"I can't believe it," Ryan said, looking at Cole. "Someone actually stood you up?"

"It's been known to happen."

Ryan's boisterous laugh fit right in at the bar that suddenly seemed too loud and too crowded for Rhett's liking. "Who stands up the heir to the Mallory Vineyard?"

"His loss is my gain," Rhett cut in, sipping his drink.

Ryan lifted his glass to his lips and drained it then gave Cole a wicked grin. "I'm cock-blocking right now, aren't I?" He grimaced and shook his head, standing up. "Don't answer that. There is so much about this that I don't want to imagine."

Rhett's mind was suddenly flooded with images that had no business being there. Images of Cole leaning in, pressing Rhett against the wall, raking his gaze down Rhett's body. It wasn't much, but it was trim, if not toned. He wasn't overly tanned, and was blind as a bat without his glasses, but in his imagination, he was enough for someone like Cole.

Rhett tried to shove the images away, but they clung to the edge of his consciousness, telling him how much better it would feel to be snuggled up to Cole when they were naked. Suddenly aware of his unintended celibate streak, Rhett blushed and wished that he could stop his current train of thought.

He shouldn't have been fantasizing about the man he was going to marry just for show. They were still going to have their separate lives, somehow. He trusted Cole to be discreet about any encounters he arranged. After all, he had more to lose if this went south than Rhett did.

His stomach soured at the idea of Cole sleeping with other people, whether it was okay with Rhett or not, or discreet or not. He chalked it up to the long strange evening he'd just had and forced himself to say a proper goodbye to Ryan, who seemed to want to be anywhere other than here.

Ryan left the bar, and Rhett watched through the windows until his silver car shot past the front of the building and vanished. He exhaled, and Cole kept his arm around him. It felt nice, so he wasn't about to argue about the necessity of it.

"This night has felt like one giant coincidence." Cole finished his drink.

Rhett pulled his glasses off and rubbed at his eyes. "I've never lied so much in my life. Is it always this exhausting?" Rhett put his glasses back on and looked at Cole, who had a strange expression on his face. Or maybe it wasn't strange; after all, he barely knew Cole.

"Can I buy you a drink, boyfriend?" Cole flashed him a movie-star smile.

Rhett wanted to say yes, desperately, because this night was bizarre and part of him believed that it might all be a dream. "I should get home," he said instead. "Can you send me the details for Kristen's wedding, dates and where you guys are staying. I need to book a vacation, it would seem."

"Don't worry about a thing," Cole interrupted. "We leave in a week and all the flights and stuff have been arranged. All I have to do is tell Mom I'm bringing a plus one and they'll take care of everything."

"I can't let you, Cole."

Cole grinned. "I'm not, my parents are. Consider it a perk."

"Like a signing bonus," Rhett remarked dryly. "Anyway, I should still get going."

"Can I give you a lift?"

Rhett opened his mouth to tell Cole that he'd be fine, but then he remembered that Cole was essentially his boyfriend now, and he should let Cole do boyfriend things like drive him home.

"I'd like that," Rhett replied, feeling as if it was the first true thing he'd said in hours.

The drive only took a couple of minutes. They didn't talk much, mostly Rhett giving Cole directions. When they pulled up in front of Rhett's building, Cole killed the engine and undid his seatbelt.

"I think I should come inside," Cole told him.

Rhett turned to him and blinked, stupidly, feeling very much like a deer caught in headlights.

"If I'm your boyfriend, people will expect me to have at least been in your apartment."

"Alright."

Rhett climbed out of the car and fished for his keys as he headed for the door. The idea of Cole in his apartment was doing funny things to him. He felt slightly feverish and a little nervous.

How would Cole see his apartment? It wasn't much, but Rhett

was happy with the way he'd decorated it with lots of black and white photography and loud accessories, bright colors splattered throughout the rooms to liven them up.

He unlocked the door and let Cole enter first, focusing on his shoes as he toed them off at the door.

"Nice place." Cole wandered slowly, examining every inch of Rhett's apartment. He stopped at the kitchen table and gently touched Rhett's fern. "Not what I expected."

"Excuse me?" Rhett said, feeling immediately defensive of his beloved Lucy.

"I thought you'd have a fish tank."

"I don't like cleaning the tanks. Plants are harder to kill, too."

Cole smiled and stuffed his hands in his pockets. "Good point." Cole looked around, then met Rhett's gaze. "Are you going to show me your room?"

"Show you my room? Are we ten?"

"No, but we're boyfriends now. There's certain things that I'll be expected to know, like what the inside of your bedroom looks like."

Rhett ran his hands through his hair, clasping his fingers together behind his head. "Why? It's not like someone is going to quiz you on the thread count of my sheets."

Cole rolled his eyes and turned on his heel, heading down the hallway. "If you don't want to do this, it's not too late to back out. We can break up and I'll find someone else to be my fake future husband."

Rhett didn't like the idea of Cole in his room, seeing his private space when he hadn't had time to prepare for it, but he liked the idea of Cole finding a new counterfeit boyfriend less. Being fake together was suddenly more appealing than being actually single.

"Ignore the mess. I wasn't exactly expecting company," Rhett said as Cole opened his bedroom door.

He knew what Cole would see. His untidy nightstand, stacked with magazines. His unmade bed because why bother making a bed when you were the only one who slept in it. His laundry, though, thankfully made it into the basket every day. Rhett closed his eyes and waited for Cole to see it.

"Oh, my God, you have a Garfield plushie. I loved Garfield."

Rhett opened his eyes, sighed, and joined Cole in his bedroom. Cole was sitting on the edge of Rhett's messy bed, holding the Garfield plushie and staring at it thoughtfully.

"Garfield was my favorite. Mom found him in a yard sale one time." Rhett cleared his throat, swallowing the emotion that instantly swelled there. He didn't talk about his mom very much. Ryan never wanted to, and it was too hard on their dad, so Rhett mostly remembered her alone.

Feeling unsteady, he sat on the bed next to Cole and stared at Cole's hands, the way they gently cradled one of Rhett's most prized possessions, fingers gently stroking the orange fur. "It took her three days to get the smell of stale cigarettes out of him. She spent hours, I think, cleaning him up with a toothbrush and soapy water."

"Your mom was always really nice to me."

"She liked you. She told me as much." Rhett took his toy from Cole's hands and stared at it for a moment, resisting the urge to crush it against his chest and hug it tight. "Ryan and I hated her oatmeal raisin cookies, but she made them anyway because you loved them. You were the only one."

The memory felt like a kick in the stomach. How long had it been since he'd been allowed to think of his mom, to talk about her with someone who knew her? Rhett forced his emotions down and pasted a smile onto his face.

"I showed you mine. Now you show me yours."

Chapter Five
COLE

Cole swallowed, his heart lodged in his throat. The idea of showing Rhett *his* was enticing to say the least. In actuality, and seemingly out of nowhere, Cole wanted to pin Rhett against a wall and fuck him into the next room. But he knew that was conduct unbecoming a future fake husband. He needed to find a way to keep his hormones in check if he wanted this thing with Rhett to work. Not to mention he had Ryan to contend with now.

"I'll show you mine tomorrow," Cole managed to verbalize, standing up and clearing his throat before taking a step into the hallway. Something about being in Rhett's bedroom made him feel a lot of things that exceeded far beyond the standard carnal thoughts he'd been grappling with all night.

"Oh," Rhett said, looking up and pushing his glasses up the bridge of his nose. He tucked the stuffed Garfield under his arm and followed Cole back into the living room. Cole looked over his shoulder and tracked his movements with a predatory intensity.

Rhett sat the stuffed cat next to the fern.

"Hang out with Lucy for a second," he whispered.

Cole furrowed his brows together. "Who is Lucy?"

"My fern," Rhett answered, so matter-of-factly Cole didn't even think to dispute the absurdity of it.

"So come over tomorrow. Early. I'll make you breakfast."

"Breakfast?"

"Yeah. We have a lot of catching up to do if we want to make this convincing when the weekend comes," Cole reminded him.

"Ryan is probably going to call me tonight," Rhett offered with a shrug.

"I'm sure he'll be calling both of us," he agreed. "That's why it's important we know the basic things about each other so people don't catch on."

"What's your favorite color?" Rhett asked him.

"Red. Yours?"

"Red," Rhett whispered. He did that reverse blush thing again and Cole shoved his hands into his pockets.

"How do you drink your coffee?" Cole asked, his voice unusually low and gruff.

Rhett's eyes flared. "Two sugars."

"Black," Cole shared.

"What time do you go to bed?"

"Late," Cole rasped. "I don't sleep well."

"I'm in bed by ten," Rhett replied.

"How domestic," Cole remarked.

He closed his eyes and took a deep breath, wanting so badly to tumble into bed early enough to fuck Rhett so he could fall asleep on schedule. Cole blew his breath out loudly, making a raspberry sound with his lips.

"I need to go," he said, producing his car keys and turning away from Rhett before his erection became visible.

"Breakfast then?" Rhett asked hopefully from behind him.

"Yeah," Cole said, not turning around. "Come by before nine."

He twisted the front doorknob and had one foot outside when Rhett's voice stopped him.

"Cole."

God, that voice.

"I've never been to your house."

Cole closed his eyes and squared his shoulders, not wanting to be rude, but really needing to get the fuck away from Rhett before he fucked everything up.

"I'll text you the directions." He dared a quick look over his shoulder at red-faced Rhett and his pet fern. "Sleep well, Rhett."

Cole closed the door behind him and practically ran to his car, pulling the door closed and banging his head against the steering wheel a few times before turning the key and backing onto the road.

He drove quickly, thankful to be back home. It shouldn't have been a big deal. It wasn't like Ryan's barely younger brother was some kind of forbidden fruit or something. But still...

Cole kicked his shoes off in the entryway and padded into the kitchen, checking the pantry to make sure he had sugar for Rhett in the morning. His phone was still sitting on the counter and seeing it reminded him he needed to let his mom know about his unexpected plus one.

He powered his phone on, ignoring the onslaught of text messages, including a handful from Ryan that he didn't dare read. It wasn't terribly late yet, so he decided to call his mom up at the main house.

"Cole," she answered on the fourth ring.

"Mother," he greeted.

"Have you come around since you stormed out of the house earlier?"

He bristled at her insinuation, "I'm going to have a date coming with me to Kristen's wedding."

"Impossible," she huffed.

"Excuse me?"

"It's far too late to add anyone to the seating chart, Cole."

"You literally cannot tell me that I need to settle down then tell me that I can't bring my boyfriend to my little sister's first wedding." Cole slid onto a barstool at his kitchen counter with a roll of his eyes.

"Cole MacKenzie Mallory!" she shouted at him.

"You're fooling yourself if you think this is going to be the only time Kristen gets married and you know it," he chastised.

"That's beside the point..."

Cole cut her off. "You're right. The point is my boyfriend is coming to the wedding with me and he'll need a flight and a seat. He obviously doesn't need a hotel room though."

"Since when do you even have a boyfriend, Cole? You didn't have one three hours ago."

"I didn't tell you I had one," he corrected, even though that was a loose interpretation of the facts.

"It's the perfect opportunity for him to be re-introduced to everyone, as my boyfriend anyway. The whole family will be there."

"What do you mean re-introduced?" His mother's voice took on a hint of concern and suspicion.

Cole swallowed, finding himself unexpectedly worried about committing so fully to this lie.

"I've gotta go, Mom. I'm needed elsewhere," he said quickly to avoid the question. "I'll call you tomorrow and we can talk more."

Before she could protest, Cole ended the call. He stared at his phone to make sure it wouldn't spontaneously combust in his hand or, worse, ring because his mom was calling him back.

When neither of those things happened, he set it down, pouring himself a fresh glass of wine before clicking into the text messages from Ryan.

Ryan: Did you know Rhett is seeing someone?
Ryan: What are you doing? You called me and then vanish?
Ryan: Where are you?
Ryan: I'm going to Tubby's.
Ryan: YOU AND MY BROTHER?
Ryan: I want to be okay with this, but I feel really blindsided.
Ryan: Why didn't you tell me?
Ryan: Can you stop ignoring me?

Cole huffed a frustrated groan and dialed Ryan's number. He answered on the first ring.

"Dude!"

"Dude," Cole repeated.

"Why didn't you tell me you were fucking my brother?"

"That's crass," Cole began. "And I didn't say anything about Rhett because it's nobody's business."

"It seems really out of left field."

If you only knew.

"It was unexpected," Cole answered, completely truthful. "But I think it's going to work."

It better work, or this whole facade would crash around them in a catastrophically painful and destructive way. Cole hoped that in the fresh light of morning, Rhett would still be okay with what they'd agreed to do.

"Do you...does... Fuck."

Cole could picture Ryan tearing his hair out at the roots.

"Does he make you happy?" Ryan finally asked.

"Yeah," Cole answered, telling the truth again. Rhett had made him extremely happy tonight.

"And do you make him happy?"

"I try," Cole answered, "I'll always try."

"And he's coming to Tahiti?" Ryan mumbled.

"Well, of course he is. He's my boyfriend." Cole was surprised again at how easily that rolled off his tongue. He had to keep reminding himself this was pretend. Rhett wasn't his real boyfriend. None of this was real.

Well, the erection between his legs was real.

He didn't want to have an erection while he talked to Ryan.

"Ryan, I gotta get going, okay?" Cole popped the button on his jeans and shoving his hand down his pants to adjust himself.

"Oh, yeah. I mean, are you and Rhett together now?" Ryan asked, a bit bitterly.

"No. He's home."

"Oh."

"So I'm going to get to bed. I'll talk to you soon though, yeah?"

"Right. Alright, dude. Bye." Ryan stumbled his way through the end of the call, hanging up before Cole could.

He laid his phone back on the counter and finished his wine, pouring himself another glass and carrying it with him to bed. He loved his house, but it was large. Far bigger than he'd ever need on his own. He'd only moved in because staying in the main house had been driving him insane. Even being in another wing, as far from his parents as he could manage, it was too close.

He was almost thirty, not thirteen, and he desperately needed that separation between them. Although, he lamented, it was mostly useless because even across the property, he'd still have these stupid familial relationship constraints around his neck.

Cole kicked out of his pants and tugged off his shirt, tossing it all into the hamper in the corner before he got into bed and turned on the fifty-two inch flat-screen that was mounted on the opposite wall. He flicked through over one hundred channels, not finding anything he wanted.

He knew he wouldn't fall asleep, though, even with two glasses of wine and as many beers in him. Cole settled on a random alien conspiracy show on the History channel, swallowing his last mouthful of wine before he settled back into the pillows and waited for sleep.

Chapter Six
RHETT

Cole's house was easy to find and hard to miss. For one person, it was a lot of house, a mansion by even the loosest of standards. Rhett felt a little self-conscious pulling up in front of Cole's fancy house in his non-fancy Honda Civic, but he did his best to keep it together.

He thought he'd wake up and want to call Cole and beg to be let out of the whole thing. Certainly it would seem sillier in the light of day. But the more Rhett thought about it, the more he liked the plan. Well, *like* was a strong word. It would be a good arrangement for them both. Cole would get to keep the vineyard that was so precious to him, and Rhett would get to launch his event planning business. With a name like Mallory attached to his, he was sure to be a success.

A pang of guilt stabbed at Rhett. He didn't enjoy the idea of using Cole, but Cole was using him right back, so it kind of balanced out. He quit stalling and walked up the slate steps and rang the doorbell. A minute later, Cole answered, dressed in a pair of jeans and plain t-shirt. It wasn't fair for him to look as good as he did, Rhett thought, as he took Cole's wordless invitation and stepped inside.

"I can't believe you've never been here," Cole said and motioned for Rhett to follow him.

"I think you must confuse me with my brother."

Cole made a choking sound. "Trust me, that's not the case."

They turned the corner and entered a large kitchen that looked as if it belonged in a magazine. Rhett guessed that half his apartment would fit in Cole's kitchen.

"I hope you like sausages." Cole took his place in front of the stove, motioning to the sausages as he stirred what looked like hash browns.

"Oh, shit. I probably should have told you. I'm a vegan."

Cole stilled and slowly turned, his mouth ajar, looking somewhat like a fish.

Rhett grinned. "I'm totally kidding. I love sausages."

Cole snapped his mouth shut and shook his head. "Figures, my future husband is a smartass."

Rhett slid a stool out from under the bar-height counter and took a seat. He watched Cole cook for a few minutes before Cole finally broke the silence.

"Shouldn't we be getting to know each other?"

"We are," Rhett assured him.

"But we're not saying anything. We should be talking about things."

"Like our favorite color?"

"Like that, yeah." Cole turned the stove off and grabbed a couple plates from the cupboard. He loaded them up and brought one to Rhett. "Salt and pepper? Something to drink? Coffee? Orange Juice?"

"Pepper, please. A coffee would be great."

Cole poured a coffee, added two sugars, and brought it to Rhett before getting his own breakfast and sitting beside him.

"There's more to getting to know someone than asking about their hobbies and their favorite song, Cole. There's the little things like when you're cooking you put more weight on your right leg than your left."

"How is that important?" Cole asked. Rhett watched him meticulously slice his sausage into even pieces.

"How is it not important?"

"It's just the way I stand."

"It's a detail about you. People aren't just the sum of their details, but it's how people are different from each other. You cut your sausages into equal portions working from one end to the other. You put more weight on your right leg when you stand. You need a fern."

"A fern?"

"Every kitchen needs a fern."

"Okay." Cole exhaled. "If we're going to get to know each other, we can do it your way, where we just hang out, but I still want to ask questions."

"That's fine. But I will veto any boring basic questions."

"The basics are important," Cole shot back and Rhett wanted to laugh at him...and also kiss the pout off his lips.

He stamped on that urge until it went away and chewed slowly, giving himself time to regain his composure. He didn't want to mock Cole's limited relationship experience or make it seem as if he knew everything. He took a breath and adjusted his glasses, then tried again.

"Those are surface things. When you spend time with someone without worrying about gathering data like a fact-finding mission, the things you do learn are more substantial, more organic."

"Do you know what I learned about you this morning, Rhett?"

"What?"

"You're a little bossy. Not overtly, but you definitely like to have your own way. And you're a bit of a smartass."

"Guilty as charged."

"So tell me, oh wise-relationship-guru, what do we do after breakfast?"

"You take me on a tour." Rhett glanced around, taking in more of Cole's house. "This place is huge. I bet you have a bowling alley in your bedroom."

"I do not." Cole laughed. "I had that taken out to make room for the swimming pool."

"Seriously, though, what do you do with all this space?"

Cole shrugged. "I don't really do anything with it. It's just space that happens to be away from my parents. That was the important thing."

Rhett frowned. "I'm sorry. I know this isn't really the ideal situation." He could have sworn he saw Cole's hand move toward his, but at the last second, he grabbed his coffee instead.

"Before we get in too deep," Cole paused and looked at him. His sage green eyes sparkled, and even the bags under them couldn't take away from his beauty. "You can back out now. I won't be mad. If you don't want to do this, or if you're having second thoughts about it."

"I'm not having second thoughts. I thought I might feel different about it when I woke up this morning, but..." *But I wanted to see you again. I wanted to smell you again. I wanted you to touch me and hold me and, God forbid, I think I wanted you to kiss me.* "I believe it's a mutually beneficial arrangement."

Rhett frowned at how cold and callous that sounded. He didn't want Cole to think that he was just using him. "I want to help you keep the vineyard, Cole. I don't want to see you lose it."

Cole nodded and they went back to eating their breakfast.

"I'm glad you're not vegan," Cole said out of nowhere a few minutes later when they stood to take their plates to the sink.

"Me too. Those sausages were excellent."

"I get them from a Polish guy. I can never pronounce his name, but his dad was taught by his dad who was taught by his dad and so on. They're fantastic."

Rhett listened to Cole talk about Polish meat while he openly gawked at the house. What little Rhett had seen of it impressed him.

"Show me your house, Cole."

Cole nodded and Rhett followed him, a step behind, taking in the details. The basic furniture with the this-house-has-been-staged-for-sale decor was present in every room. The room Cole called his office had a hint of personality, if you could call a cluttered desk personality.

"You need a fern."

"I thought you said my kitchen needed a fern."

"I take it back. Your office needs a fern. And at least one family photo. It's like a law or something."

"I don't want a picture of my family in my office." Cole wrinkled his nose.

"Then get a plant."

"My room's next door."

"Oh, good." Rhett grinned. "I can't wait to see the swimming pool."

Cole opened his bedroom door and Rhett entered first. The pool was only noticeable because of its absence, but the bedroom was exactly how he pictured Cole's room would be. The thick curtains let in a scant amount of light, giving the burgundy bedcovers an extra romantic feel. The dark burgundy, paired with an espresso-colored sleigh bed and matching dressers, gave the room a masculine vibe without Rhett feeling as if he were choking to death on testosterone.

"This is really nice," Rhett said as he made his way over to Cole's bed and sat down. "Oh, my God. This is heaven." Rhett flopped back and closed his eyes wondering if he'd ever been that comfortable. "How do you even leave your bed?"

"You find bed to be less appealing if you rarely sleep."

"Wouldn't that make bed more appealing?"

The room went deathly silent and Rhett felt his face heat to a point near volcanic temperatures. He hoped that Cole couldn't see how red he'd turned. He couldn't believe he'd made a sex joke while lying on Cole's bed. Cole, who probably wouldn't ever want him like that. Rhett stood up and cleared his throat. He wasn't supposed to be thinking about Cole and his bed and how much he wanted to be in it with him. This was all supposed to be pretend; why couldn't his attraction take the hint?

"We should schedule some time together before the trip," Cole said. "An apartment tour and one breakfast date does not a fake relationship make."

"What did you have in mind?" Rhett asked, feeling suddenly nervous when Cole looked at him and grinned.

"It's a surprise."

"I want to say that I love surprises, but I really don't."

"You'll love this. Trust me. Have I ever steered you wrong before?"

"Not me, no." Rhett folded his arms over his chest. "But there was that one time you and Ryan were joyriding in your dad's golf cart and you drove straight into a water hazard."

Cole's grin fell and he scowled at Rhett, the humor still present in his eyes. "I don't know if I'm going to like having a boyfriend who knows all the stupid shit I've done."

"You'll love it. I already know all the dumb stuff you've done so your family can't bring out the stories and embarrass you."

"That's a good point."

"Good enough for you to tell me what the surprise is?"

Cole grinned. "Nope. You'll have to be a good boy and wait."

Rhett sighed. "It was worth a try."

Chapter Seven
COLE

※❦※

Cole had no idea what he was going to show Rhett, but he needed to get him out of his bedroom and out of his bed. Before he realized what he was doing, he reached behind him and laced his fingers into Rhett's and pulled him into the hallway. Cole stumbled on his way into the living room and Rhett slammed into his back, the heat of his chest noticeable through their clothes.

The kitchen counter looked like a good place to fuck Rhett. So did the couch. Cole needed to get him out of the house. He yanked Rhett toward the front door and onto the porch, leading him around the driveway and into the vineyard.

"I've never been down here like this," Rhett said breathlessly.

"These are cabernet grapes," Cole told him, plucking one from a bunch and rolling it between his fingers.

"They're small," Rhett observed.

"They're late bloomers. They're not quite in season yet." Cole pulled him deeper into the vineyard.

"It smells really good," Rhett said, inhaling deeply.

Cole inhaled also, but didn't notice anything out of the ordinary.

"Does it?" he asked, looking over his shoulder to Rhett, who was wide-eyed with wonder at the vines surrounding them.

"Do you not smell all the grapes?" Rhett laughed and squeezed Cole's hand.

All Cole could smell was Rhett.

"I guess I'm used to it," he answered, emerging from a short row of vines near the back of one of the vineyard's private tasting rooms.

Cole dug his keys out of his pocket and unlocked the door, pulling Rhett inside behind him. He flipped the light switch on the wall, illuminating the intimate room, decorated with display oak barrels and industrial-style chandeliers with brushed bronze finishings.

"Sit," he told Rhett, pointing to one of the plush beige chairs situated around a low, unfinished wood table in the center of the room.

Rhett sat, running his palms back and forth across the soft upholstery. Cole ducked behind a small bar against the back wall and grabbed two bottles of wine, tucked one beneath his arm, and then took two glasses from under the bar and carried them back to the table.

Cole sat in a chair opposite Rhett and pulled a bottle opener from his keyring, slicing the foil seal on one of the bottles before popping the cork out. He did a three-ounce pour into each of the glasses and pushed one across the table to Rhett.

"Okay, so no boring questions," Cole repeated Rhett's demand from breakfast.

"Right."

"Then start drinking." Cole tipped his own glass toward Rhett before taking a sip himself.

"What?" Rhett sputtered.

"If we're drunk, it's less likely to be boring."

Rhett took a small drink, his face looking pained. Once the wine hit his tongue, his features softened and he followed up with a larger swallow.

"You like?" Cole asked, feeling particularly proud.

"Yeah." Rhett nodded.

"It was my favorite year," Cole told him, taking another drink and encouraging Rhett to do the same.

The merlot they were drinking was almost seven years old. It was from the first year Cole assumed management of the vineyard. He might have been biased about the flavor, but nothing they'd produced since then tasted better to him.

"There's another thing I know about you," Rhett said proudly, leaning over the table and pouring himself another glass. Cole cleared his throat. He hadn't even realized that Rhett had drained his first.

"What's that?" Cole was genuinely curious. He shifted his weight, aware that he was resting more on his right hip than the left.

"You're so proud of this place." Rhett smiled loosely.

"I don't think we'd be here if this place wasn't important to me."

Rhett rolled his eyes. "Not just important. That's not what I said. It's like you don't listen when I talk."

Cole raised his eyebrows.

"I said you're *proud* of it," Rhett repeated, gesturing with his glass before taking another drink.

"I have one about you," Cole countered.

"What have you figured out, Mr. Future Fake Husband?" Rhett sassed.

Cole licked his lips, adjusting himself again, but more because of uneven blood distribution than uneven weight distribution.

"You're a lightweight." He tipped his chin down and saluted Rhett with his glass.

"No, I'm not," he protested, shoving his glasses up his nose and back into their proper position.

"What's your favorite way to pass the time?" Cole asked, changing the subject.

"Reading." Rhett smiled at him, a bright and beautiful thing.

"What do you read?"

"Everything," Rhett exhaled his answer and finished his wine.

Cole reached between them and picked up the merlot, pouring a few more ounces into Rhett's empty glass.

"Why event planning?"

Rhett scoffed at him, "Why *not* event planning, Mr. Mallory? Oh! Cole Mallory. I'm Rhett Kingston. When we get married, do we hyphenate? Whose name goes first? Mallory-Kingston or Kingston-Mallory? I'd never try to say that you should take my name, but Mallory-Kingston does seem to roll off the tongue a little easier, don't you think?"

Cole was one more hyphenated last name away from kissing Rhett into silence.

"Rhett Mallory-Kingston?" Cole questioned, finishing his wine.

Rhett blushed from his cheeks down, and Cole almost pointed it out as an observation that he'd made, but decided against it. He wanted to keep it to himself for a little longer. It was a secret for his knowledge only.

"I like it," Rhett breathed.

Cole jumped out of the chair and walked over to the bar, bracing his hands against the edge and dropping his head.

"Maybe drinking before lunch was a bad idea," he mumbled.

"What?" Rhett asked.

Cole heard Rhett's glass clink against the table, followed by him shuffling across the small room and lingering just behind him.

He could feel Rhett there, already accustomed to the way heat radiated out from Rhett's chest through the rest of his body—the way it set Cole's blood on fire.

"You're drunk," Cole replied, not turning around.

"So?" Rhett stepped closer. His chest couldn't have been more than a foot away from Cole now.

"It doesn't matter, you know," Cole turned to face Rhett. "About the names. It's pretend. You don't even need to change your name if you don't want to."

Because it'll be easier for you when we get divorced, Cole added silently, the meaning of his statement clear either way.

Rhett frowned slightly and closed the few inches between them. Cole closed his eyes and took a steadying breath. Rhett reached for his fingers, twining their hands together.

"People need to think it's real."

Rhett's breath was hot against his face now, their palms sweaty against each other.

"I don't know about you, Cole, but I'm not the kind of person who would get married and not take my husband's name in some capacity."

Rhett squeezed his hands and Cole looked down, staring at the way their fingers twisted together at their sides.

"Mallory-Kingston, then," he confirmed.

Rhett made an agreeable sound in his throat.

"Cole Mallory-Kingston."

Rhett was far too close to his mouth. The air in the room was gone. Cole couldn't breathe, couldn't think. All he knew was Rhett's hands were in his, their hips were aligned, Rhett's mouth hovered over his, exhaling names from a future that wouldn't ever really exist.

Ideas that Cole hadn't ever had before about anyone, let alone Rhett, sparked in his brain like out of control fireworks. Hyphenated surnames and shared bank accounts. Spring in the vineyard. All things that he couldn't ever have. This arrangement with Rhett was just a tease, a taunt of things that were just out of his reach.

"Rhett," he managed to say his name. "Please don't do this."

"Why not?" Rhett asked, so close now that Cole couldn't be certain their lips weren't touching. Rhett's breaths were his breaths.

"It's a bad idea." Cole swallowed.

"But people will know."

"What will people know?"

"If we haven't been intimate." Rhett breathed into Cole's mouth, the deep fruit taste of the merlot was rich on Cole's tongue. "There's a sort of familiarity between people who've been inside each other."

Cole's cock pressed against his thigh and in a move he wasn't sure he wouldn't regret for the rest of his life, he shook free of Rhett's hands and stepped aside.

"You've been drinking," Cole reminded him.

Rhett turned, resting his butt against the bar and watching Cole retreat back to the table they'd been at earlier.

"I have. I am, you know, at a vineyard." Rhett gestured to the room they were in.

Cole chuckled, debating another glass of wine for himself.

"What is it like?" Rhett asked him, eyes narrowed.

Cole decided he needed more wine and topped off his glass, emptying the bottle. "What is what like?"

"Being with you. Like that."

Rhett pushed off the bar and slinked back toward the table, dropping into his chair while holding his eyes on Cole.

"I don't know what you mean," Cole managed to reply, even though he was pretty sure he knew exactly what Rhett was asking.

"How do you fuck, Mr. Mallory-Kingston?" Rhett asked, far lewder than Cole had ever seen him before.

"Do you want to know how I've fucked everyone else, or how I'd fuck you?" Cole asked, unable to bolster himself against the intensity of Rhett's stare any longer.

"Me."

"With you, Rhett, I'd take my time."

Chapter Eight

RHETT

It was probably the best merlot he'd ever tasted, but he doubted it could compare to how Cole would taste. Rhett felt hot all over, a side effect of the wine perhaps, or maybe it was a side effect of standing so close to Cole. Close enough to taste his breath, and Rhett wanted to taste the rest of him.

Cole, however, was honorable. Not honorable enough to not get an erection, though. Rhett had noticed the bulge in Cole's jeans; it matched the one in his, and it inspired a thousand filthy ideas of things he'd like to do with Cole.

Rhett wanted to know things that he'd never needed to before, and the prospect of being Cole's husband thrilled him in a strange way. Standing before him was a gorgeous man. A gorgeous man Rhett knew to also be a kind and generous man. And he suddenly wanted to know how Cole moved in bed. He wanted to know how Cole would look, sweaty and spent, draped over him. Rhett couldn't picture it and he needed to. He needed to know what kinds of things his husband would do to him.

If he'd ever choose Rhett like that.

The best merlot he'd ever tasted emboldened him and he found himself asking Cole questions he'd never been brave enough to ask before. Heat swept up Rhett's body, radiating from the center outward when Cole pinned Rhett in place with nothing more than his gaze. Rhett said the words over in his head, imprinting them there, doing his best to remember the sexy way they'd tumbled out of Cole's mouth.

With him, Cole would take his time. Rhett wished then that he wasn't a lightweight and that Cole actually meant it, that he wasn't in this for reasons of his own, just like Rhett was. Were it not for the strangeness of their current situation, would Cole have even thought twice about him?

"I think getting me drunk before lunch was a very bad idea," Rhett said, watching the way Cole watched him. It wasn't fair that Cole could move so fluidly, so steady on his feet, when Rhett's limbs felt like lead weights and his brain chugged along at half capacity, making booze-fueled decisions and giving him wine-tinted ideas about Cole fucking him slow, taking his time just like he'd said.

Cole was suddenly there in front of him and Rhett smiled as he watched him open a bottle of water and hand it to him. "Drink up, babe. If you hydrate, you'll feel better."

Rhett smiled again and took the water from Cole, taking a small sip. "I have been drunk before, Mr. Mallory-Kingston."

Rhett loved the way their names sounded together. He loved the idea of hyphenating their names. Taking something that belonged solely to Cole and solely to himself, and making it into something that belonged to both of them.

"Will you let me have a bottle of the merlot?" Rhett asked. When they finally got what they both wanted and parted ways, he could drink it and remember that Cole never stopped to smell the grapes and that Cole's hands felt like the best thing he'd ever held.

"Whatever you want."

What Rhett wanted, he couldn't have, so he nodded. "Show me something else," he said, lacing their fingers together. "Maybe something with a lower alcohol content or I'll be dead by dinnertime."

"I'll keep your low tolerance in mind for when we're in Tahiti."

Rhett grinned like an idiot—he knew he did—but he couldn't help it. "I know the reason I'm going is to try and sell this..." He couldn't bring himself to say the word fake again, so he dodged it. "This thing between us, but I'm a little excited for Tahiti. I've never been." Rhett stilled. "I just realized I have nothing nice enough to wear to a wedding. And I'll need new swim shorts. And luggage." Rhett started compiling a list in his head of everything he'd need to buy and do before he left for Tahiti.

Cole tugged Rhett toward the door. "Let's go shopping. I can help you pick out something nice for the wedding."

"I'm two-point-one sheets to the wind, Cole."

"Then you better let me drive," Cole said as he dropped Rhett's hand long enough to pull the door shut and lock it. Rhett's stomach fluttered nervously when Cole grabbed his hand again.

"This is the weirdest first date ever," Rhett said as he followed Cole. "Breakfast. Drunk before lunch. Then shopping."

"Drink your water. You'll regret it if you don't."

"Yes, dear." Rhett smiled at Cole, knowing the wine made him looser than he'd normally be. He wanted to know if he could feel this comfortable without fermented grapes chugging through his bloodstream.

Rhett loved shopping, sober. Half-drunk, being tugged from store to store by Cole, forced into changing room after changing room, proved to be exhausting.

"Forget dinner. I barely made it to lunchtime," Rhett said when Cole slid into the driver's seat after stowing Rhett's bags in the trunk. "I need a nap."

Rhett gently removed his glasses and rubbed his eyes with his free hand before putting them back on.

"Lunch then?"

"Not sick of me yet?" Rhett put his hands in his lap. He'd wanted to touch Cole all day. They held hands a lot and Rhett told himself that he was only reaching for Cole so they could get used to it, to make it believable for when they had to fake it in front of his family.

"I could never get sick of you." Cole blew Rhett a kiss, then started the car.

Rhett didn't turn his phone on until he was home alone, much later than he'd anticipated. Breakfast with Cole had turned into an entire day together. It was now after dinner and Rhett had just set all his purchases for Tahiti out on his bed. The bottle of wine that he'd asked Cole for sat on his dresser next to Garfield. The sight of it there did funny things to his stomach. Needing a distraction, he turned his phone on and wasn't surprised at all to see several missed calls.

He called his best friend, Penny, telling himself that he'd call Ryan back later.

She answered, practically screaming in his ear. He put the phone on speaker and tossed it on his bed.

"I can't believe you didn't tell me! You and Cole Mallory. Since when?"

"It's new." Rhett made a point to keep as close to the truth as he could. "Ryan told you?"

"He called here trying to pump me for information. I can't believe you've been banging Cole Mallory and kept it to yourself."

"We wanted to wait before telling people." Rhett wished he could busy himself with packing, but he needed to wash the new items first. He stared at the outfit Cole had helped him pick out for the wedding. Kristen wanted people dressed smartly, Cole had said, handing him a pair of trousers with a matching jacket and a white button down. Cole had picked out a set of matching ties for them to wear.

"I'm not people, Rhett; I'm your best friend."

"Penny, I'm sorry, but I don't tell you everything, you know."

She scoffed. "I know that. Lucy's the only one you really pour your heart out to."

Rhett looked at his bed, at the spot where Cole had sat while

Rhett talked about his mom. He didn't respond to Penny and she changed the subject from his love life to motherhood.

She tried to tell him things to gross him out, but Rhett wasn't bothered by any of it. Plugged milk ducts, projectile vomit, diaper explosions, none of it bothered him, and Penny declared him a spoilsport. It wasn't any fun to tell him all the disgusting things if he was unaffected, but that didn't stop her from trying.

"Are you listening to anything I've been saying, Rhett?"

"Um. No. Sorry." Rhett laughed. "I was trying to think if there's anything else I need to bring."

"Bring where?"

"Tahiti."

"Tahiti?"

Rhett facepalmed. "I'm going to Tahiti with Cole for Kristen's wedding."

"Wow. You don't mess around, do you? One minute you're single and the next you're going to Tahiti for your secret boyfriend's sister's wedding," Penny giggled. "Condoms. Bring lots of condoms."

"Condoms. Got it."

Rhett did not have it. Not even a little.

"Trust me. Bring extra. That's how David and I ended up with little Tyson."

"I don't think I'm in danger of getting pregnant, Penny."

"Better safe than sorry." In the background, little Tyson started to fuss. "I have to go and see if I can get him down for the night. You better bring me something back from Tahiti."

"Well, it won't be Cole's bun in my oven. I'm not plumbed like that." He didn't tell her they weren't sleeping together. Not for lack of trying on his part. Rhett smiled a little when he thought of Cole and the moment they'd shared. Their hands linked, their hips lined up, close enough to kiss, and the heat in Cole's eyes had Rhett hoping that he, in fact, did turn him down because Rhett was drunk and not because Cole didn't want to kiss him.

"Har har." Penny shushed her fussy baby, who was growing louder and angrier by the second. "I have to go. Love you." She hung up before he could say goodbye.

Rhett stared at his empty suitcase and wondered if he *should* pack condoms...just in case.

Chapter Nine
COLE

"Are you ready for this?" Cole asked Rhett after he'd stowed his suitcase in the back of the car. Rhett slid into the passenger seat with a tiny *oomph*, and his eyelashes fluttered before he managed to make eye contact.

"I mean, I've got to be," he answered.

"The flight shouldn't be too bad. The seats are two in a row and we have the back so no one will really be able to see us."

"Unless they turn around."

"Well, that would be just sort of rude and creepy, don't you think?" Cole questioned.

The airport was close and he drove them to one of the on-site, long-term parking lots. Once parked, Cole pulled his and Rhett's suitcases from the trunk and wheeled them toward the entrance.

"I can carry my own bag," Rhett offered, but Cole shrugged him off with a tip of his chin.

"If you were really my boyfriend, I wouldn't let you."

And that was the truth. Rhett's bag was heavy as fuck and Cole wasn't convinced he hadn't somehow packed Lucy in there, but he was raised to be a gentleman and treat his partners well.

"What if *I* wouldn't let *you*?" Rhett asked him. "What if I wanted to play the part of chivalrous and attentive boyfriend? What would happen then?"

"Are you the chivalrous and attentive type?" Cole responded, very aware that he needed to know, for reasons far beyond maintaining the charade.

"I'm attentive," Rhett responded, his voice noticeably scratchy. "I like to make sure my partners have what they need."

Cole hoisted their bags over the curb in silence, passing them off to a curbside porter and taking the claim tags.

"Are we still talking about luggage?" he asked.

Rhett looked the slightest bit deviant as he angled a look toward Cole. "What else would we be talking about?"

"Cole!" His mother's shrill voice echoed through the airport ticketing area. He took a deep breath and looked in the direction her voice had come from. Rhett stilled beside him.

"Where's this mystery plus one of yours? Kristen was furious when I told her, by the way. Oh, hi Rhett, you traveling today?"

"He is," Cole answered for him, ignoring the rest of his mother's greeting. "With me. Rhett and I are seeing each other. He's my plus one."

Cole stretched his fingers, grazing against Rhett's wrist. Rhett snatched his hand, quickly threading their fingers together like they'd been doing it for months.

"What?" she sputtered, eyes darting between their faces before dipping down to their now joined hands.

"Cole and I have been dating, Mrs. Mallory," Rhett contributed, putting a dazzling smile on display.

Cole was transfixed.

When he'd spent the past week thinking about how he couldn't wait to share a bed with Rhett, he now feared it. He wanted Rhett with an unmatched ferocity and he didn't know how long he could control himself before he ruined the entire thing.

Cole made a mental tally of things he'd have to avoid over the coming week in order to not blow their cover. No unnecessary affection, no excessive drinking—for him or for Rhett. And definitely no bed sharing. Cole would sleep on the couch. Or he'd build a divider out of towels and pillows, or *something*, because while he knew he had to keep his distance from Rhett, the idea was completely unappealing.

"Since when?" his mother asked, brows knit in speculation.

Cole swallowed, aware that this wasn't one of the things they'd discussed. Rhett had been so intent on cataloging Cole's idiosyncrasies that neither of them had thought about coming to an agreement on the finer details that everyone would be asking them.

"Not long," Rhett answered for him. "Only since June."

Cole made a mental note.

"Really, Cole? Since *June* and you didn't say anything?" his mother balked.

"First of all, it's not anyone's business. Second," Cole lowered his voice and turned his attention to Rhett. "We liked having it be our little secret."

Rhett's nostrils flared and his lips parted. Cole made another note of the fact that Rhett's brown eyes looked gold in this light then he turned back to his mother.

"And, as you are well aware, circumstances now require that it not be secret. So, now you know."

His mother looked tired.

"Circumstances require you get married, Cole, not have a boyfriend."

"Well...who knows, Mother." Cole's heart fluttered. "We're going to go now. Time to get through security and get to the gate before boarding."

"I have to wait for your father. We'll see you at the gate." His mother glared at her phone.

"It was good seeing you, Mrs. Mallory. I'm excited for Kristen's wedding. Thank you for inviting me." Rhett cast another dazzling smile at his mother and Cole pulled him away, their hands still joined.

"Since June, then?" Cole asked once they were through security and settled into seats near the boarding gate, but not close enough that they'd be within earshot of family.

"I just picked something plausible," Rhett answered with a shrug.

"I know you didn't want to do the mundane getting to know you, but we should go over it apparently," Cole reminded him.

They spent the hour wait going over anything they agreed could be a necessary piece of information in case they were interrogated separately by anyone in Cole's prying family.

After they boarded their flight, rows behind Cole's parents, Rhett settled into his seat and rested his head against the window.

"Are you all right?" Cole asked, leaning into his space. Rhett looked...not sad, but maybe mournful? Cole couldn't pinpoint the feelings that skittered across Rhett's cheekbones. He was pretty sure if they'd been dating since June, though, he'd have been able to.

"Fine," Rhett answered, a smile on his face that Cole was seventy-four percent sure was forced.

He knew he had *just* instituted his own don't-touch-Rhett-unless-you-have-to rule, but he had to. He raised his hand slowly, tracing his fingers over Rhett's cheekbone. The worry on his face melted away.

"See, I'm fine," Rhett repeated, more convincing this time.

"Alright," Cole conceded, relaxing back into his own seat.

After the flight attendant went through the safety checks and the wheels of the plane left the ground, Rhett pulled an e-reader out of his carry-on.

"Do you mind if I read?" he asked.

"Not at all. But you have to tell me what you're reading." Cole grinned. He unrolled his headphones from around his phone so he could plug them into the seat back screen and watch a movie while Rhett read.

"It's a romance."

"Are you getting ideas?" Cole asked, teasingly.

Rhett reverse blushed in that adorable way he did.

"No," he answered quickly.

"Would you read to me sometime?" Cole asked, not entirely sure where that question had even come from.

"I mean, if you want, I guess," Rhett stammered.

"I'd like that."

Cole pictured a vineyard spring morning, tucked into bed with Rhett under his arm reading aloud while he drank his coffee. An impossibility.

"Sometimes they get kind of raunchy," Rhett whispered. "Not this one, but sometimes there's, like, a lot of sex."

Cole pictured a crisp fall evening, tossing Rhett's book aside and pounding into his plump little ass after hearing a particularly inspiring excerpt. Another impossibility.

He jammed his headphones into the jack and put the buds into his ears. Rhett seemed to take the cue for what it was, flipping the cover on his reader back and beginning to read.

Halfway through Cole's movie, Rhett's head landed against his shoulder. He arranged himself like this was a position they were familiar with and resumed his reading.

When the credits rolled, Cole pulled his headphones out in time to hear Rhett mumble, "You're such a flirt, Eroch."

"Who is Eroch?" he questioned.

"Huh?" Rhett asked, pulling back and looking up at Cole in confusion.

"You said something about Eroch." Cole told him.

"Eroch is a dragon."

"You're reading a romance about dragons?" Cole asked, now even more befuddled.

"No. That's an entirely different genre."

"I'm so confused." Cole laughed, shaking his head.

"You're particularly handsome when you don't understand something," Rhett whispered, dragging a thumb up the bridge of Cole's nose. "You get so squinty."

Cole's eyelashes fluttered at Rhett's touch and he sucked in a sharp inhale.

"Sorry," Rhett said quickly, pulling his hand away and tucking it into his lap. "That was probably inappropriate."

The only thing inappropriate was how *not* inappropriate it was, but Cole kept that thought to himself.

"I feel like we should have some rules," Cole forced himself to say. The words were bitter on his tongue, but so necessary. Rhett wanted his business and Cole wanted his vineyard, so this had to work.

Rhett looked around the first class cabin, eyes landing on Cole's parents a few rows ahead of them before he returned his attention to Cole.

"Be quiet," Rhett warned him.

"But don't you..."

Rhett cut him off. "We don't need rules. We just need to not do stupid things."

Cole swallowed. "You're right."

A flight attendant appeared beside him, leaning down with a soft voice and a smile.

"Can I get you gentlemen some lunch? We have a baked chicken with pineapple and coconut or we have a steak sandwich."

"My boyfriend is vegan," Cole said with a smirk.

"I am not!" Rhett smacked his chest in protest.

Cole's mother turned at the commotion and he grabbed Rhett's fingers and held them against his heart. It was thundering against his ribcage and he knew Rhett would be able to feel it. He only hoped his nervousness and his want didn't read as such to Rhett.

"The steak," Rhett ordered.

"I'll have the same," Cole concurred, unable or unwilling to let go of Rhett's fingers, even after the attention of his mother and the flight attendant were gone.

"I never order chicken," Rhett said untangling their hands.

"It's never cooked right," Cole mumbled.

"Exactly!" Rhett agreed proudly. "We are a match made in fake boyfriend heaven, aren't we?"

"We are."

They flipped their tray tables down when the attendant came back and Cole ordered himself a glass of champagne. He downed it and asked for another, ready to pace himself once the bubbles were flowing through his blood.

"I have a confession," he said to Rhett conspiratorially.

"I do love a good truth," Rhett remarked, licking some *au jus* from his thumb.

"I love wine. Obviously. But I really love champagne."

"Why doesn't Mallory make some then?"

"Technically, champagne is only champagne if it comes from a specific region in France. Everything else is just bubbly wine."

"Well, let's be honest. Champagne is just bubbly wine with a higher price tag," Rhett countered, leaning over and taking a drink from his glass.

Cole noticed the imprint of Rhett's lips on the glass and he tried to not stare at it for fear of an airplane boner.

"I think Mallory Bubbly Wines has a really great ring to it," Rhett told him.

Cole was inclined to agree. In fact, that was something he'd thought about in the past. Not specifically branding something as bubbly wine, but coordinating a marketing campaign to target his generation more than his parents'.

Mallory was a long-running vineyard and a well-established name, but wine was still widely considered too complex to younger people, the variations and types too obtuse for the normal person to make sense of.

Mallory Bubbly Wines could be the flagship bottle under a whole new branding. The wheels in Cole's head were spinning full speed.

"Have you ever been to France?" Rhett asked, breaking his concentration.

"Of course," Cole answered with a shake of his head. He made wine. Of course he'd been to France.

"Oh," Rhett replied, tucking into his seat and leaning a

shoulder against the window. "Not all of us have had the same opportunities as you, Cole."

Cole felt like an asshole. Well aware that Rhett and Ryan's parents had always worked. Even though they owned their rental company, their dad had thrown himself into work completely after Rhett's mom died. They'd never had the sort of wealth the vineyard and their family money had provided Cole and Kristen.

"I'll take you," Cole blurted. "We can go drink wine in Bordeaux. Whatever you want."

Fuck. He wanted that future. That impossible and fraudulent life.

"Don't be ridiculous, Cole," Rhett hissed, crossing his arms over his chest. "I'm not your boyfriend."

Chapter Ten

RHETT

Cole nodded and Rhett had the distinct impression he'd somehow hurt Cole's feelings, but the notion was absurd. Everything about this relationship was pretense and Rhett had no right to be dreaming of vacations in France that belonged to Cole and a real boyfriend.

He smiled at Cole and reached for his e-reader. Desperate to do anything but sit there and feel awkward. By the time Rhett thought of something to say, Cole had fallen asleep next to him. His head tilted toward Rhett, as if he'd been watching him read.

Turnabout was fair play, Rhett supposed, and he switched his e-reader off in favor of watching Cole. Even in his sleep, he was unfairly handsome and blessed with thick, long lashes that lay in dark fans against his cheeks. Rhett's gaze drifted down to Cole's five o'clock shadow and his fingers twitched as he restrained himself from touching. He needed to know things about Cole. Things he could keep with him when all of this was over. Things like the way his stubble felt under Rhett's touch, or the way his eyes fluttered slightly as he woke.

Cole's eyes opened and Rhett swallowed thickly as Cole's

expression warmed. He opened his mouth to protest, somehow, that he hadn't been watching Cole sleep like some creeper.

The flight attendant chose that moment to inform the passengers that they'd be making their descent into Tahiti in ten minutes and that it was time to make sure their seatbelts were fastened and they were ready for landing.

Cole let Rhett get off the plane first, but was quick to link their hands together as they joined up with his family and headed toward the luggage carousel.

Rhett sidled up closer so he could whisper to Cole, "They keep looking at me."

Cole laughed. "I think they're shocked. That's all. By the time we get to the hotel, they'll be either too drunk or too tired to pay much attention to us. Plus, they have bridezilla over there to wrangle."

Rhett exhaled. Being drunk sounded both very good and very dangerous. He recalled the tasting room and the nearness of Cole, the way their bodies had lined up perfectly. He let go of Cole's hand, allowing him again to be a gentleman and get Rhett's bag. It was unfortunate that he wasn't Rhett's actual boyfriend. Even though they were faking it, Cole had been nice to him so far and they'd had a lot of fun talking and hanging out in the week before the trip.

Rhett veered out of dangerous territory and followed Cole out of the airport and onto a bus that took them to the ferry. By the time they boarded, Rhett was bone tired. "I never knew travelling was so exhausting. I could sleep for a week and all I've done is stand, sit, and wait."

Cole put his hands on Rhett's shoulders and kneaded the muscles with his fingers. "When we check into the hotel, we can hide in our room and order room service."

Rhett wanted to groan out loud at how good Cole's hands felt on his shoulders. "Aren't we here for a wedding? Isn't your family expecting us to hang out with them?"

"We're free the rest of today and tomorrow. The day after is the rehearsal, then the day after that is the wedding. And the day after that is hangover day to recover before we fly home the day after *that*. We'll need to be there for the rehearsal stuff and the wedding. That's it."

Cole's arms wrapped around his waist and he rested his chin on Rhett's shoulder. The sunlight glinting off the ocean was almost as blinding as the sudden swell of fondness he had for Cole in that moment.

"There you two are," Cole's mother said as she approached, her heels clicking on the deck of the ferry. She looked at Rhett and offered a smile, more decorum than affection Rhett thought, before looking to Cole. "Will you two be joining us for dinner tonight?"

"Afraid not, Mom. Rhett and I are pretty tired. We're going to take it easy in the room tonight, but we'll join you for breakfast."

His mom waved a manicured hand at Cole, dismissing his suggestion. "No, thank you, dear. You're up far too early for me. Lunch, perhaps, if you're around?" She looked at Rhett and this time Rhett thought her to be genuine when she smiled. "It's nice to see you, Rhett. I do hope we get a chance to catch up."

Rhett feared they'd be trapped on the boat forever, making small talk with Cole's mom, but her phone chimed and she pulled it out of her purse. "This wedding is going to kill me," she moaned as she tapped out a text.

"Not if you kill Kristen first."

"Cole, there will be no talk of murdering your sister before the wedding. It's bad luck."

"Since when?" Cole shot back. He moved away from Rhett and was no longer blanketing his back, but he kept his arm around him the whole time, marking territory that wasn't really his.

"Your sister is a menace," his mom complained. "She needs me for something. I swear to God, three months is not a long enough honeymoon. I'll see you boys later."

"Nice seeing you again, Mrs. Mallory."

She turned. "Please, Rhett, call me Constance." Her phone chimed again and she rolled her eyes. "Duty calls."

Alone again, Rhett was free to take in his tropical surroundings. "It looks just like it does in the pictures," he breathed, admittedly feeling somewhat awestruck.

"You sound surprised."

"You know how it is. You see a picture of a hamburger on a menu, and you order it, and it's not how it was pictured? Or you order a shirt online and it looks great on the site, but doesn't look good on you? This is the exact opposite of that." Rhett knew he was grinning like an idiot, but he couldn't help himself. "Thank you for this, by the way."

It felt like an eternity before they arrived at the hotel and Rhett was thankful for Cole, as he leaned against him in the hotel lobby, taking advantage of the fact that everyone thought they were together.

Cole smoothed his hand down Rhett's back. "You okay, babe?"

"I'm fine. I don't know whether I want to lie down and sleep or go for a swim. Traveling is hard." Rhett added a bit of extra whine to his last phrase, which made Cole smile.

"We can do both. We'll check into our room, change into our swim trunks, then get a cabana at the beach. You can swim, then nap, or nap, then swim."

"You are the best travel partner ever." Rhett winced internally as he thought of France, and Bordeaux, champagne, and the vacation that would never really be his.

Their room, once they finally were in it, was beautiful. Crisp white linens framed the windows and Rhett walked over to them, drawn to the view of the ocean just outside. He opened a set of doors that led straight out onto the small deck and then the sand. He snapped a few quick photos with his phone and sent the images to Penny and Ryan. Penny was quick to respond with an immediate *I hate you*, and a half a dozen heart emojis.

Rhett heard Cole handle the luggage and the tip. He'd have

offered, but Cole had a thing about being chivalrous, and Rhett rather liked feeling taken care of, so he decided to let him.

He turned around, grinning, feeling far more refreshed than he'd felt all day. "This place is beautiful. And that bed is huge. Is it a California king or eastern king size do you figure?"

"It's an eastern king." Cole said simply, unzipping his luggage.

"So, swim, nap, eat, or eat, nap, then swim?" Cole pulled out a pair of turquoise trunks.

"Um. I think we can just wing it, can't we?" Rhett abandoned the view in favor of finding the trunks he'd brought. Rhett unzipped his suitcase, slowly, suddenly aware of the fact that there was only one bed in their hotel room. Which made sense, of course, they were boyfriends after all, sort of.

Rhett grabbed his trunks out of his suitcase and spared Cole a quick glance as he hurried toward the bathroom. "I'll go change in here," he said, trying hard not to let on how spooked he suddenly felt.

He shouldn't be so freaked out, Rhett admonished himself once he was alone. He'd had hookups before he had gotten naked in front of. He'd woken up to a one night stand using his chest for a drool bib. Certainly he could be a grown up and change in front of his fake boyfriend. Or share a bed with him. He didn't know what he was so terrified of when all of this was pretend.

Rhett changed, splashed some water on his face, and forced himself to ignore the giant bed-shaped elephant in the room and focus instead on getting into the water as fast as possible.

He opened the bathroom door and nearly choked on his tongue. Cole in clothing was gorgeous, but Cole in nothing but a pair of trunks was hot as hell. Unfairly hot. His body was lean and tight and had a maturity that it certainly didn't have the last time he'd seen Cole Mallory in a pair of swim trunks so many years ago.

"You ready?" Cole asked, reaching for Rhett.

Rhett took Cole's hand. "For anything," he answered.

Chapter Eleven
COLE

❦

Cole pulled Rhett out the sliding glass door and onto their private strip of beach. The sand and sun were warm, the breeze off the water was thick with humidity.

"We should bring the fruit," Rhett said as his feet hit the beach.

Cole doubled back and grabbed the complimentary fruit plate off a small table on the deck and chased after Rhett.

"Here," he gasped, catching his breath and holding a strawberry up to Rhett's pink lips. The way he shaped them into an O and puckered his mouth before sinking his teeth into the skin of the strawberry bordered on obscene, and Cole had to close his eyes, lest he shoot off in his swim trunks.

"That's so ripe," Rhett enthused, lifting a finger to his chin and swiping at some dripping strawberry juice.

"They grow pineapple here," Cole shared, picking a spear from the plate and taking a bite. He wasn't even really a fan of pineapple, but Tahitian pineapple was delicious—far sweeter and juicier than whatever they could get at the store back home. And besides, there was that rumor it made your...well, it didn't much matter if it made anything taste better because no one was going to be tasting anything.

No matter how much he wanted to taste or to be tasted.

"Fuck, the water is so warm!" Rhett called to him, already yards beyond Cole and up to his waist in the water.

Cole set the plate in the sand and splashed into the water behind Rhett, tackling him from behind and slamming them both face first into the waves.

"Oh, my God!" Rhett sputtered, struggling to stand and wiping his hair out of his face. "I wasn't expecting that."

"That's what makes it fun," Cole reminded him. He returned to the shore, dropping into the sand and using his finger to slide the fruit around the plate. He popped a couple grapes into his mouth and leaned back, watching Rhett frolic in the water, wading deeper into the calm sea.

⁂

Hours later, after the sun had dipped lower in the sky and they'd both showered and dressed again, Cole sat across from Rhett at a small seafood restaurant tucked into the tropical forest about a mile off the hotel property.

"How did you know this place was here?" Rhett asked, eyes wide in awe.

Cole looked around the restaurant. It was a humble place, owned by a local and it looked like the restaurant used to be, or maybe still was, their primary residence. The dining room opened into a garden decorated with half a dozen wooden tables and plastic patio chairs. It served the best seafood he ever had.

"I've been here before," Cole said, reaching for his beer and taking a small drink.

"Oh, of course," Rhett said, his eyes squinting together before he quickly shifted his attention to the plastic checkered tablecloth.

"Why do you say it like that?" Cole asked. "You're upset."

"What makes you think I'm upset?" Rhett answered back quickly, eyes still narrowed.

"You squint. Like, not just a normal squint. I don't know how to explain it." Cole was pretty sure he was blushing. His cheeks seemed warm and he didn't think it was just the humid air.

Rhett's face softened then, noticeably, and Cole couldn't help but smile.

"Two steamers," the hostess slash waitress slash owner said, setting two large, wicker steamer baskets down in front of them before disappearing back into the house.

"You didn't answer me," Cole said, pulling the lid from his basket.

"It's just easy to forget that we're so different," Rhett whispered, toying with the lid of his basket.

"I didn't think we were," Cole said, a little upset by the implication of Rhett's words. "How do you mean?"

"Well, come on, Cole." Rhett gestured around them. "We're on an island in the middle of the ocean at a restaurant that looks like a house and I've never even been out of California, but you've somehow already been to this house-restaurant?"

"Just on a vacation before."

Rhett exhaled and pulled the lid off his basket. "I've never been farther than San Diego."

"Well, now you have. And we're here together, and I want you to eat this dinner with me, okay?" Cole slid his hand across the table, palm up. Rhett looked down at his upturned palm but didn't move.

"Rhett," Cole whispered, bending his fingers. "You're my boyfriend. Hold my hand. Drink this beer. Eat this dinner. With me."

Rhett's throat turned pink and he slowly placed his palm against Cole's. Their fingers slid against each other, skin hot and damp from the tropical air, or something else entirely.

"It's pretend," Rhett rasped, jawline and cheeks turning red to match his throat.

"Alright," Cole agreed, twining their fingers together. His breath caught in his mouth and he made a best effort to commit the angles of Rhett's muscles to memory—from the thin lines of his fingers to the slight bulge of his forearm up to his trembling bicep.

"But it still needs to be believable," Rhett murmured, squeezing his hand.

Cole's heart stopped—he was sure of it. Rhett licked his lips and Cole's cock was thick against his thigh. This was too much. This was dangerous. He took his hand away.

"We should eat before it gets cold."

And just like that, the moment passed.

Cole and Rhett ate greedily, their fingers and hands dripping with juice and butter before they'd even gotten halfway through their meals. The woven baskets, upon being opened, overflowed with shrimp, fresh blue crab, oysters, clams, whitefish, fruit, and vegetables. Everything tasted a little bit like everything else while still maintaining its unique texture and flavor. The shrimp was Cole's favorite; it always had been.

"I'm so glad you're not vegan," he said again, pulling a genuine smile from Rhett's butter-slick mouth.

"God, me too," he agreed, sucking a finger between his lips with a wet pop.

Cole reached for his beer and drank what he estimated to be half the bottle in one swallow, slamming it back onto the table a little louder than he'd intended. The waitress appeared on cue and set two fresh bottles beside his empty.

"They drink booze like water here," Rhett remarked, finishing his beer and popping the top on the new one.

"It's true. Bottled water is the only water you should drink on the island and it's actually more expensive than beer depending on where you go."

"It's like they want you to come here, get drunk, and make mistakes or something," Rhett laughed and stabbed at something in his basket with a fork.

There was a lot of things Cole wanted to do here, but he was less and less convinced that any of them would really be a mistake.

"What other food is good here?" Rhett asked, blissfully unaware of Cole's illicit train of thought.

"Uhm, pretty much everything you'll eat that's not from the hotel," Cole shared. He had two pieces of pineapple left in his basket and he ate them for good measure before putting the lid back on and setting the entire thing aside.

"Are all the restaurants like this?" Rhett waved his hand behind his head.

Cole slid his beer closer to his body, picking at the label with his thumbnail.

"No. Well, the good ones." Cole smiled. "There's a place a little way down the road that is set up like a traditional Tahitian village and they do these extravagant dinner shows where they roast a pig and everything. The food there is good, but it's a bit more touristy, if that makes sense."

"I mean, isn't this whole island touristy?" Rhett questioned with a tilt of his head. "I don't see any local people sitting down and eating dinner with us."

Cole looked around, noticing that Rhett was correct. "You're right," he agreed, finally getting a nail under the edge of the label on his beer and giving it a good pull.

"It's not bad or anything," Rhett hastily amended. "I just noticed is all. This whole place is, what did the concierge say, a fifty kilometer loop? I can't imagine there's many ways to make a living here if you don't work at the hotel or turn your house into an impromptu dining establishment."

"I honestly never even thought about that."

Rhett smiled and picked up an oyster, tilting his head back and sucking it straight down his throat. Cole watched the way the muscles in Rhett's jaw and throat moved, then looked away and took another drink of his beer.

"The beer is good here, though," Rhett changed the subject, lifting the bottle to his mouth after he'd finished the oyster.

"It's a bit watery," Cole noted.

Rhett smiled and took a big drink, raising his eyebrows and setting the now empty bottle on the table. "That's how they get ya."

The waitress was there again, like magic, leaving two more bottles before them, plus a bill, and collecting their empty steam baskets.

"Do you want to walk back to the hotel?" Cole asked, checking the total and pulling money out of his wallet to leave in payment.

"Can we take these?" Rhett asked, lifting his bottle in the air.

"No one is going to tell us no. Come on."

Cole pushed his chair back and collected his bottle, waiting for Rhett to join him.

"*Maururu!*" Cole said, raising his bottle toward the waitress.

"*Maeva nana*," she returned with a wave.

"What the fuck?" Rhett asked with a hearty chuckle, following Cole onto the sand and grass covered strip of land that served as a sidewalk.

"*Maururu* is thank you in Tahitian. *Maeva nana* is, like, thanks and bye."

"Hmn." Rhett took a quick drink of his beer and fell in line beside Cole as they began the walk back to their hotel.

"What do you think so far?" Cole asked him, chewing on the corner of his lip, thankful for the dark so Rhett wouldn't see the nervous tic.

"About?"

Me.

"The island," he answered.

"Oh, it's lovely. Honestly, it's all a bit surreal."

Rhett's fingers bumped his hand.

"Holy shit!" Rhett shouted, jumping backward and curling his arms around Cole's shoulder and waist, using him as a human shield for…something.

"What?" Cole laughed, looking around and not seeing anything of note.

"There's something in the bushes!" Rhett pointed just ahead of them and, on cue, the bush shook with movement. "We're in a tropical forest. Oh, God, I don't even know what kind of animals live out here."

Cole laughed, and patted Rhett's hand reassuringly. "Did you not study up before the trip? I'm honestly surprised."

"I didn't have a lot of research time before we left," Rhett reminded him. "I was with you."

The way Rhett's voice dipped at the conclusion of his sentence made it sound like their spending time together mattered a lot more than it should have. But it could have also been all the beers they'd had. Cole set the thought aside.

The bush moved again and Rhett squealed, using Cole's shoulder to hide himself from whatever lay in the leaves.

"It's a crab, babe," Cole said, finally putting him out of his misery and fear as a small blue crab crawled out of the bushes and side-stepped across the road.

"A what?" Rhett asked, reaching on his tiptoes and looking over Cole's shoulder.

"A crab." Cole unfolded Rhett from behind him and pointed at the crab. "We're on an island. There's crab everywhere."

"Oh, God." Rhett bent at the knees and took a deep breath. He looked to the side and searched out Cole's face, a look of utter mortification across his features.

"I'll protect you from the errant street crabs. Don't worry," Cole promised, extending a hand toward Rhett. He took it, their fingers twisting together in that perfect way again. Rhett bumped his shoulder into Cole's and made an embarrassed sound.

"Can we never talk about this again?" he pleaded.

"Oh, we're going to talk about this for a long time," Cole countered with a laugh.

They walked the rest of the way back to the hotel, hand in hand. Cole listened to the sound of the water from the other side of the street and the steady pace of Rhett's breathing until they reached the hotel grounds, where it hitched and stuttered.

"Are you okay?" Cole finally mustered the courage to ask as he slid the key into the door of their hotel room.

They walked into the room and the door closed behind them, automatically locking. He and Rhett stood in the doorway, hands still entwined, Rhett's breathing even heavier than two minutes ago.

Cole followed Rhett's gaze to the corner where it was solely focused on the single king-size bed that they were about to share.

Chapter Twelve

RHETT

Tahiti was a dream. A wonderful, too good to be true dream that starred Cole Mallory, suave fake boyfriend of the geeky, and suddenly slightly tipsy, Rhett. The sight of the one bed in the room made Rhett's head spin. Okay, so maybe a little of the spinning his head was doing was related to the beer he drank at dinner.

"It's just a bed, Rhett." Cole spoke quietly, as if afraid of spooking him.

Too late. Rhett took a deep breath. "It's a lot bigger than my bed at home."

"I know."

Cole's words reminded Rhett of how it had felt to have him in his room, sitting on his bed. He'd felt exposed, but not in a bad way. He felt much the same way now. Like Cole had the ability to look at him and actually see him, and the spark of interest Rhett pretended he saw in Cole's eyes sometimes fueled his desire to let Cole in, to open himself up. Something about Cole made him feel safe and it was that feeling he clung to now, just as tightly as he held Cole's hand.

"I'm going to get ready for bed." He finally dropped Cole's hand, rummaged through his suitcase for his bag of toiletries, and slipped into the bathroom. He could scarcely breathe through the tightness in his chest. It felt dangerously domestic, this dream vacation. Eating on the beach. Playing in the surf, feeling Cole's gaze on him the whole time. Dinner. Being saved from the crab, and now Cole stood in the next room while Rhett took a piss and brushed his teeth.

Cole had always been Ryan's friend. One of the guys. Ryan talked endlessly about the things they did and the fun they had, and Rhett had never been jealous. He had his own life and his own friends, and he wouldn't trade Penny for anything. He didn't feel jealous now, but just a new kind of warmth inside. He had these new memories with Cole, memories that were his and Cole's alone. It sounded stupid, even to himself, but he didn't want to tell anyone about them; he feared they'd seem less magical if he spoke about them.

A knock on the door jarred him out of his thoughts. "You okay in there?"

"Yeah, be right out." Rhett laughed and finished brushing his teeth. He left his bag of toiletries on the counter and exited the bathroom. "I didn't mean to take so long, I guess I zoned out."

"More tired than you thought?"

"Something like that." Rhett smiled and was thankful that Cole couldn't hear the way his heart raced or feel the dampness of his palms. "I'm going to turn in." Rhett's gaze slid over to the bed.

"I could sleep on the floor. Or in the chair. I can't believe this room didn't come with a couch."

"Cole, no. It's fine. We're adults. We can share a bed."

"Okay." Cole smiled at him. "I'll be right out."

Once he disappeared into the bathroom, Rhett stripped his clothing off and tucked himself into bed. He normally slept naked, but tonight he decided that it would be a good idea to leave his boxer briefs on. He lay on his side, facing the ocean, and hoped that he'd miraculously fall asleep before Cole joined him.

Rhett quickly discovered that sleeping would be impossible if he didn't get his heart rate down. With every second that ticked by, he felt more awake. The knowledge that he was about to sleep next to Cole had breathed a second wind into him.

The bathroom door opened and a moment later the other side of the bed dipped down as Cole climbed under the covers.

Then...

Nothing.

Rhett inhaled, closing his eyes, imagining that he could smell Cole's toothpaste, the salt on his skin, and the clinging aroma of Tahitian beer.

"Rhett?" Cole's voice was scratchy and far too intimate. It felt like a caress in the dark hotel room. A moment Rhett stole and called his own, tucking it away with all the other things he'd never tell anyone.

"Yeah?" He answered back.

"If you don't stop being awkward about this, I'll sleep on the floor."

"I'm not awkward." The bed moved a little and Rhett had the distinct impression that he was being watched.

"Then why are you clinging to the edge of the bed?"

Rhett rolled onto his back and looked at Cole, who was far too handsome in the dim light. "Sorry. I'll try to curb myself."

"Please do. It would mean a lot if you could save it for the next time we're out and you're attacked by a gang of errant street crabs."

Rhett felt himself blush all over again. "Are you gonna make this a thing? It could have been anything."

"But it wasn't. It was dinner. You were scared by lunch on legs." Cole laughed, his tone affectionate.

They dissolved into laughter and Rhett discovered that the weirdness was gone. In its place was a comfortable silence, filled only with friendship. He supposed it wasn't a bad thing, to enjoy spending time with his fake boyfriend. Rhett snuggled down into the covers, wiggling a little to find the perfect position. He cracked an eye open and found Cole looking at him.

"Good night, Cole."

"Good night, Rhett."

Sleeping with the curtains open meant Rhett was up with the sun. He watched his first foreign sunrise snuggled in bed, trying to deny that he'd wanted to wake up in Cole's arms and not just in the sheets. It would've been an accident, and maybe it would have made things even more awkward, but it had been a while since he'd had the chance to cuddle with someone. Rhett wasn't sure exactly what the dynamics of their fake relationship would be, but he hoped to one day negotiate cuddle time. He didn't think Cole would be opposed to the idea.

"Good morning." Rhett heard Cole mumble behind him and the bed shifted around. "What do you want to do today? It's our only day of freedom before the wedding stuff happens."

Rhett rolled over, abandoning the view of the sunrise to look at Cole, who happened to be gorgeous, all sleepy-eyed and messy-haired. "I don't know. You're the expert. What do you suggest we do?"

Cole yawned and stretched, and Rhett did his best to not ogle his bare chest. "We could take a boat to a private island. We could go horseback riding. We could swim with the sharks."

Rhett squeaked. "Definitely not."

Cole grinned, wide and beautiful, the corners of his eyes crinkled. "I'd keep you safe, you little fraidy-cat."

"You can keep me safe by not taking me to swim with sharks. That sounds like the least safe thing we could do together." Okay, the second least safe thing, Rhett thought, hoping Cole would get out of bed first and give him time to tame his raging hard-on. It wasn't a normal morning erection; it was one fueled by Cole's sleepy face and the fantasy of doing nothing all day but lying in bed with him, just like this.

"Okay, no sharks." Cole flung the covers back and climbed out of bed, stretching his arms above his head as he yawned. "I'll grab a shower. Did you want to get room service or go somewhere to eat?"

Eating in the room sounded far too intimate for Rhett and the runaway fantasies in his head. "Is anything open right now?"

"Something's always open," he replied as he rummaged in his suitcase. "Out in a few."

Rhett lay in bed while Cole showered, contemplating breakfast, and trying not to think of a very naked Cole in the next room, water cascading down his body and soap sliding down his skin. Rhett climbed out of bed and pressed his hand down against his erection, willing it to deflate. Sharing a bed with Cole had been as bad of an idea as he thought it would be.

When Rhett heard the bathroom door open, he hurriedly grabbed a change of clothes. "I won't be long," he told Cole as their paths crossed.

"Take your time."

Rhett shut the bathroom door and tossed his clothes on the counter before padding over to the shower. He turned it on and adjusted the spray before stripping out of his underwear and stepping under the water.

He contemplated turning the cold water on and taking care of his problem a different way, but Cole was under his skin now. Even alone in the bathroom, it was as if he could feel Cole's presence twining around him, becoming part of him.

Rhett wrapped his hand around his cock and bit back a groan. He flattened his other hand against the tile and closed his eyes. Water alone proved to be a little rough against his skin, so he stopped long enough to use some body wash to slick his movements.

He at least tried to think of anything besides Cole, but it felt wrong to think of anyone else when the person he really wanted, *but shouldn't*, stood in the next room waiting for him. So Rhett let himself think of Cole and the way their hands felt so perfect together; the way he'd touched Rhett's cheek, or bumped his shoulder. Each memory stole Rhett's breath and soon he was biting back a moan as his orgasm slammed into him, leaving his legs shaky.

He finished his shower and hoped that one orgasm would be enough to keep his suddenly revived sex drive at bay until he could be alone again.

Then he left the bathroom and knew he was doomed. Cole tucked his wallet into his back pocket and held his hand out for Rhett to take. "Ready?"

"For anything except sharks," Rhett replied, taking Cole's hand, blushing a little when he remembered what he'd just used that hand for.

"You're smiling," Cole remarked with a raised eyebrow.

"Of course I am. I'm in Tahiti." Rhett hoped Cole wouldn't press and was thankful when he smiled, as if he somehow knew, but chose not to say anything.

Chapter Thirteen
COLE

"This is unbelievable."

Rhett stretched out on the sand of an uninhabited beach a few miles off the coast of Moorea. Cole glanced over at him and watched him bury his toes in the sand and wiggle them until they were visible again.

"What specifically?" Cole asked, kicking a spray of sand on the top of Rhett's foot.

Following a quick wank in the shower and some deliberation after seeing Rhett's apprehension to being in the same water as a dozen harmless sand sharks, Cole had booked the island boat tour. They were with a group of three other couples—real couples—and after they'd all helped the tour guides prepare lunch, they'd split off to enjoy more secluded parts of the beach before they were due to return.

The sun was just beginning its descent toward the horizon, the air smelled like tiare flowers and roast pork, but all Cole could see was the way the light bounced off Rhett's golden skin; all he could smell, the subtle hint of sweat that had broken out on his neck.

"I mean, it's beautiful." Rhett turned and smiled at Cole and the sweat slicked further down his neck into the dip of his throat.

"And it's crazy to think that a place like this exists. Such a gorgeous stretch of land that nobody lives on, and with this view."

Cole followed Rhett's gaze as it drifted toward the crystalline blue ocean a few yards beyond where they lay.

"It is lovely," Cole agreed, studying Rhett's profile.

There was no way he was going to make it through the week.

"This is probably the wrong venue, but I think there's some things we need to talk about," Rhett said suddenly, turning sharply and adjusting his position in the sand. Cole reacted accordingly, brushing stray grains of sand and shell from his legs.

He desperately hoped Rhett wasn't going to call him out on the huge erection he'd been sporting when he got out of bed this morning. He'd tried to untangle himself from the covers and turn quick enough that his crotch would be obscured, but if Rhett had caught a glance of his inappropriate boner, this whole deal could be shot.

"Have at it," Cole said with a forced smile.

"I've been thinking and there's some logistical things we need to agree on."

Cole let out the breath he'd been holding.

"Like what?"

"Like, when are you going to propose to me, for one?" Rhett asked.

Cole's eyebrows lifted toward his hairline. "You're direct."

"Yeah, well, I'm your future fake husband, so get used to it."

Cole narrowed his eyes at him. "You're a lot meaner than your brother, you know."

"Did you want to fake-marry him?" Rhett teased him, flicking sand off his knee.

"Definitely not." Cole cleared his throat, displeased with how gruff his answer had sounded.

"Seriously, though. We need to have a schedule, or at least, like," he stopped and twisted his face into a grimace. "I don't know, Cole. We need to know how long we're doing this for, don't you think?"

Cole did think. He thought about a lot. Primarily, he thought about how his life would be a living hell being fake married to Rhett and not able to *really* fuck him for however long was necessary.

"I want to make all your dreams come true," Cole answered, and he was surprised to find that the words rang true in his heart. He swallowed and shook his head, offering Rhett a sincere smile. "If I was really your boyfriend, I'd know how you want to be proposed to, so tell me that."

"Christmas." Rhett scoffed at himself. "That's so trite."

"No it's not. Tell me," Cole pushed.

"I love those cheesy Hallmark Christmas movies," Rhett admitted, "and I always wanted it to be like that when someone proposed. Cheesy Santa hats, Christmas tree, yummy smelling candles, twinkle lights."

"Does Lucy get twinkle lights too?"

His head snapped up so quickly, Cole was surprised there wasn't a noise that went along with it. Rhett's eyes were wide and focused on him, then they narrowed as they scanned across his features.

"What does Lucy have to do with this?" he asked.

"She's your plant, baby. I just assumed she'd be there," Cole stammered.

There was a short silence before Rhett answered, "When I think about it in my head, she's there."

"So, there's your answer." Cole scratched at the back of his head. "I'll propose to you on Christmas Eve, at your place. We'll have hats and mulled wine from the vineyard, and Lucy will have her own lights."

Rhett made a disagreeable sound.

"No?" Cole questioned, not sure of where he'd gone wrong.

"If we're serious enough to be getting married, don't you think we would be living together?"

Cole was going to be dead before New Year's if Rhett kept dropping all this logic.

"That's more romantic." Cole tested the idea. "The winery is beautiful at Christmas. I'll decorate appropriately and make sure Lucy is festive for the occasion."

"Alright," Rhett agreed, "Thank you for that."

"For what?"

"For trying to give me my dream proposal even if it's fake."

Rhett's face always did this pained looking twitch when he talked about their pretend relationship and it made Cole feel physically ill. The idea that anything he said or did being responsible for causing Rhett any discomfort made him ready to call the entire thing off until he came up with a better solution. Or worse.

"We should stop that. You should stop, I mean."

"Stop what?" Rhett angled his head.

"Saying it's fake. We can't slip up and say that where someone could overhear. So you just shouldn't say it anymore."

Rhett's features softened and his lips quirked into a small smile. "Alright."

"That's settled then," Cole finalized and Rhett nodded in agreement.

"That sort of comes around to the other thing I wanted to talk to you about, which is starting my business." He looked nervous and Cole patted him on the knee until he smiled again.

"What do you need from me to get started?" he asked.

"I'm not sure."

"That's easy. I'll get you in touch with someone from the winery marketing team when we're home from the wedding."

"Are you serious?" Rhett's mouth fell open.

Cole reached forward and placed his finger on the bottom of Rhett's chin, pushing upward to close his mouth.

"Of course I'm serious."

"I was thinking I could plan our wedding," Rhett blurted, before slamming his eyes closed.

"I assumed you would." Cole shrugged. Rhett's life goal was to be an event planner. Cole was supposed to help him start the business. Planning their wedding had seemed to Cole like it was a given.

Rhett launched himself forward, his arms wrapping around Cole's shoulders with such force he fell backward into the sand. Rhett landed on top of him and the air whooshed from his lungs. Cole didn't dare move, he just lay there, his back on the hot sand and Rhett's chest plastered against him.

"Thank you," Rhett exhaled. "Thank you. Thank you."

"You're welcome," he responded, his lashes fluttering closed when Rhett's breath danced across them.

Another silence. Another moment of stillness between them. Cole tried to memorize the weight of Rhett's body on top of his before he locked it in a mental vault and tried to focus on end of year financials for the vineyard so his cock didn't stab Rhett in the thigh.

"You're squishing me," he lied.

"Fuck. I'm sorry," Rhett apologized, scrambling backward.

Cole waited a beat before returning himself back to a sitting position.

"Oh, you're a mess," Rhett lamented, reaching forward and brushed his hand down Cole's chest. "Sand everywhere."

Cole's nipple hardened under Rhett's inconsequential touch, and he cursed himself.

"Five minute warning, everyone!" the skipper of the boat called out to them, ready to board so they could return to the main island.

Cole shook his head and pulled away from Rhett's touch.

"We should get back to the boat," he said.

"Yeah." Rhett stood and brushed the sand off them both, shuffling toward where the boat was docked.

Cole followed him, allowing his eyes to linger on the firm globes of Rhett's ass under his swim trunks. He'd use the sandy beach as an excuse to take a shower when they got back to the hotel and he'd just have to jerk off again.

"Where do you want to get married?" Cole asked him after

they'd settled into their seats on the boat and had begun the short journey back to the hotel.

Rhett bit his lips between his teeth and stared at the waves lapping against the bow of the boat. He didn't answer. Cole reached between them and grabbed his hand, gripping his fingers securely in his own.

"Did you want to get married here?" Cole guessed. "Because we can. We can come back here. I don't care."

He'd spare no expense for Rhett; he knew that already.

"Not here," Rhett whispered, a blush spreading up to his forehead.

"Tell me." He pulled Rhett closer, his shoulder bumping into Cole's chest. Rhett relaxed against him, their sweaty and sandy skin sticking together. Cole took a risk and wrapped Rhett in his arms, his fingers sliding tentatively across Rhett's stomach and chest.

Rhett's heart slammed against Cole's hand, but neither of them acknowledged it.

"Tell me," he repeated, his lips hovering near Rhett's ear.

He rolled his head against Cole's chest and turned, his breath puffing against Cole's chin with even measures as the boat bounced across the sea.

"I've always wanted to get married at Mallory." Rhett's admission landed hot and true against Cole's mouth.

Chapter Fourteen

RHETT

Once again, the difference between his and Cole's realities reared its ugly head and Rhett came to an abrupt halt as the table came into view with the two empty chairs waiting for them. The rest were filled and Rhett recognized only a handful of the people. Cole's parents, his sister, and his grandparents were all familiar to him. It blew him away that everyone else here could afford to fly to Tahiti for a wedding.

Cole squeezed his hand and whispered his name, "Rhett. It's okay."

Rhett looked at him, feeling more than a little out of place. "I feel like I'm about to go in front of the firing squad."

Cole laughed. "They're not that bad, come on." Cole tugged him toward the table. He smiled at everyone, offering them a cheery greeting and pulling Rhett's chair out for him. "Sorry we're late, everyone. I could have sworn that Mother said rehearsal lunch, not brunch."

Rhett took a seat and tried to act as natural as possible, but he suddenly felt as if everyone at the table were staring at him. Desperate for a distraction, he looked at Kristen. If anyone loved taking center stage, it was her.

"You look lovely this morning, Kristen. Tahiti agrees with you." Rhett felt like an idiot for saying it, but Kristen beamed and she flashed him a terawatt smile.

"Aren't you the sweetest?" She turned to her fiancé, her blonde curls bouncing. "See? I was right. A tropical wedding was the best option. We're going to have gorgeous photos."

Rhett was thankful that the conversation at the table started up again. Cole poured Rhett a glass of orange juice and he drank half in one gulp.

"Cole, you never told us you were serious about someone," Cole's father, Malcom, said suddenly, his authoritative voice stilling the surrounding conversation.

Cole reached for the tongs and grabbed a couple of sausages, plopping them onto Rhett's plate before he served himself. "I don't tell you a lot of things, Dad. Rhett is my business. Our relationship was on a need to know basis. I wanted him to come to Tahiti with me for Kristen's wedding, therefore, you needed to know."

Rhett wished he had something to contribute to the conversation, but Cole's dad made a sound in the back of his throat that Rhett translated as disbelief or maybe irritation. Possibly both.

The weight of Cole's hand on his leg was an anchor. Cole squeezed Rhett's knee and leaned over, brushing his lips against his ear. "Relax. Eat something," he whispered, then kissed his cheek.

His skin felt as if it were on fire and were it not for the stares of the people at the table, Rhett would have reached up and touched his cheek to see if he could feel the remnants of the kiss on his fingertips.

He managed to glance at Cole, feeling somewhat sheepish because of the kiss, and was met with a radiant look on Cole's face. *But Cole was always radiant, wasn't he?* Rhett turned his attention to his food.

They ate in peace for a few minutes, but then the conversation circled around back to the two newest lovebirds at the table. "How is it that the two of you ended up together? Cole has been a confirmed bachelor for as long as I've known him." The question came from Kristen's fiancé, Edward.

Before he could stutter a response, Cole draped his arm over Rhett's shoulders. "Edward, it's your rehearsal meal; why don't you let Kristen tell us all how the two of you met?"

Rhett appreciated the way Cole kept the spotlight off of them as much as possible and the way he handled his family with such a practiced ease.

His remark to Edward seemed to have steered the conversation firmly away from them and back to Kristen, who more than willingly absorbed the attention that made Rhett uncomfortable.

It might not have been so bad if everything wasn't a performance, Rhett thought as he poked at his eggs. If he could relax and not worry about slipping up and blowing the whole charade, he'd probably be having a great time right now. He'd always liked Cole's family, and he'd honestly been having the best time with Cole the past week. But there was too much at stake, he realized, frowning at his plate. If he blew it, Cole would lose the vineyard and he'd never forgive Rhett.

Rhett would never forgive himself.

"Are you all right, dear?" Cole's mother asked him, her brows pinched with concern.

"I'm fine."

Cole squeezed his shoulder. "I've kept him pretty busy. He's never been to Tahiti before so I've been trying to show him all the sights in the time we have to spare." Cole glanced at Rhett and must have sensed his discomfort. "There's actually more I want to show him. You don't really need us at rehearsal, do you, Kristen?

"God, no," Kristen scoffed, taking a sip of her drink. "We don't need you or your towel boy, Cole, honestly."

"Towel boy?" Rhett questioned, head tilted.

Kristen waved her hair in the air, giant engagement ring catching the light. "That's what your family does, right? Like, the washing?"

Rhett's face heated and he opened his mouth to reply, but Cole cut him off. "His parents own a party rental company, you idiot. Don't be rude."

Kristen's eyes flared. "Weren't you going? Besides."—she rolled her eyes—"Sandy will be too distracted if you're here."

Sandy gasped and tried to swat Kristen's arm, but she shrieked and dodged, nearly climbing into Edward's lap to get away.

"I hate you." Sandy's voice was shrill, but not unaffectionate.

Kristen stuck her tongue out at Sandy, then looked at Cole and made a shooing motion with her hand.

"I wouldn't mind if you and your boyfriend stuck around," Cole's grandmother said icily. Rhett had only met her a couple times, and she'd never been a particularly warm woman. He guessed that Kristen took after her quite a bit. "I wanted to get to know this young man."

Rhett felt himself shrink under her gaze.

Cole set his napkin on the table and laced his fingers together with Rhett's. "Sorry, Grandma. We'll have breakfast with you and Grandpa, once we're home." Cole pulled Rhett to his feet.

"Cole, really, do sit down," his mother implored, but Cole shook his head.

"Sorry, Mother, this is Kristen's week. What she says goes. And she said, so we go."

Kristen agreed with Cole again, the disdain dripping from her words indicating she was angry that Rhett had received even the slightest bit of notice at an event that should be all about her. Rhett never had liked Kristen very much, but he had to admit to a small shred of gratitude for her large personality and her ability to redirect everyone's focus.

Cole led him away from the table and Rhett grinned, happy to escape.

They walked fast, nearly jogging until they were out of sight, then Cole slowed and looked at Rhett. "She's a pain in the ass, and I'm going to get her for that shitty towel boy comment, but I can't complain that I have you all to myself again."

Rhett's cheeks flamed as he thought of the kiss on the cheek

Cole had given him at breakfast. "It was nice of her to give us an out."

Cole rolled his eyes. "She wanted me out of the way because we were stealing the attention. And with me out of the way, she can behave however she wants."

"You keep her in line or something?"

Cole glanced at Rhett. "I have dirt on her. Lots. It's what brothers do."

Rhett thought of his relationship with Ryan, which was far different from Cole's relationship with Kristen. "Not all brothers."

"Oh, come on. Surely there's something about Ryan you could use against him if you had to?"

Rhett thought, but only long enough to decide that even if such a thing existed, he wouldn't use it. "I wouldn't do it," he said out loud. "No matter what I thought it would gain me. It wouldn't be right." He looked at Cole. "What do you have on her?"

Cole grinned. "Nothing, actually. But I tell her that when I inherit the vineyard, I won't let her have her big fancy anniversary parties there."

"You're devious."

"I am."

"Okay, so now you've got me all to yourself, what are we going to do with our sudden freedom?"

Cole grinned a wicked grin and tightened his grip on Rhett's hand. "We're going to a bachelor party."

"Edward's?" Rhett frowned, confused.

"God, no. Ours."

"Ours?"

"Yes, ours."

"We're having a bachelor party before you propose. Isn't that a little backward?"

Cole's laughter caught Rhett off guard. "Yes, it is. But nothing about this situation is normal, Rhett. You don't want rules, and that's fine, but that means that I get to make things up as I go along."

Rhett nodded, dumbstruck by the heat in Cole's gaze. "Okay, Cole. Bachelor party it is."

"Perfect. You won't regret this."

※

The evening sand held as much heat as the afternoon sand, Rhett thought to himself as he stared out at the horizon, his head pleasantly fuzzy. He wasn't drunk, but he'd been riding the same buzz for hours, coaxing it back to life without crossing the line into nearly wasted like he'd done at the vineyard.

Cole had been right. He hadn't regretted a single moment that he'd spent with him that day. They wandered the island, hand in hand like real boyfriends. They'd done a little shopping. Rhett picked out a set of turquoise bracelets for Penny, a set of matching Bora Bora t-shirts for her husband and their son. For his brother, Rhett grabbed the ugliest coffee mug he could find, a garish red with Tahiti scrawled across it in a fancy font with plenty of curly tails. Ryan would hate it.

Cole purchased a couple things while Rhett was busy picking out Penny's gift. They made it back to their room and put their purchases away. Cole, taking pity on Rhett and his tired legs, suggested they stick to their own little section of the beach and order room service.

That's how Rhett found himself lying in a lounge chair, full of crab, seafood, and beer, his body boneless and warm in the last vestiges of the sun. He let his head roll to the side and he stared at Cole, who looked out at the ocean.

Rhett was getting close to developing real feelings for his fake boyfriend, he realized. Dangerously close. Rhett tore his gaze away from Cole, as Cole glanced at him, catching him.

"Your idea of a bachelor party was pretty tame, I have to admit."

Cole took a sip of his beer. "My partying days are behind me for the most part. Besides, the day was nearly perfect. Don't you think?"

Rhett hummed his agreement and stared at the horizon.

"Tired?" Cole asked a few minutes later, his voice sounding thick and delicious. His mouth probably tasted like beer and his skin probably smelled like sunshine. Rhett had no business thinking about those kinds of things.

"Yeah. A little. But I want to stay out here a while longer." Rhett watched the waves lap the shore, tinted red from the Tahitian sky.

"Whatever you want, Rhett."

He nodded, unable to make himself answer Cole's words. He thought they sounded like a promise and he allowed himself to think of them that way until the sun sank down under the ocean and took its colors away.

Chapter Fifteen
COLE

Cole woke slowly, a persistent ache in his arm that wouldn't quite go away. He rolled his shoulder to try and get the blood flowing, freezing in place when he realized the cause of the discomfort.

Rhett.

More specifically, Rhett lying on top of his arm because his entire body was tucked against Cole's side. The more Cole woke, the clearer everything became, from the warmth of Rhett's skin to the hot dampness of his breath as it landed against Cole's side.

He reached his free arm down, brushing Rhett's hair out of his eye so he could see his face. How had he never noticed how handsome Rhett was? He'd spent his whole life within reach of Rhett, and his ferns, and his books, and his gentle caresses, but he'd never noticed him. Never *stopped* to notice him.

How on earth would anyone compare to Rhett after this facade was over? Cole hadn't even had a taste of Rhett; he didn't know what his breath smelled like in the morning and he didn't know what his face looked like when he came. But here he was, angling to marry the man. Yeah, it was for show, for his livelihood, for Rhett's livelihood. But Cole would be lying if he didn't admit the whole thing seemed like a shit idea the further into it they got.

Rhett groaned and Cole immediately mourned the anticipated absence, only to be met with relief when Rhett settled closer against him. Rhett's eyelashes spread like a fan, long curls normally hidden by the lenses of his glasses.

Cole dared to reach between his legs, shoving the heel of his hand against his erection to try and quell it. Unsuccessfully. There was no hope for him on an island vacation with a handsome man who made him laugh and who was now wrapped in his arms, even if it was unintentionally.

"Mmmn," Rhett moaned and the sound shot straight to Cole's dick. He swallowed and tried to ignore it. Rhett angled his hips toward him, rubbing his cock against Cole's hip. He moaned again and Cole grabbed the sheets between his fingers, anything to avoid flipping Rhett over and pounding him through the mattress.

"Rhett," he whispered, hoping his voice would rouse him enough that he'd roll away on his own.

Rhett skated his hand up Cole's stomach, fingers sliding into the dips of his muscles and ribs as he slid up Cole's chest. Cole's heart rate accelerated, slamming like a caged bird against his sternum.

"Rhett," he tried again.

"Baby."

Cole scrubbed a hand down his face, angry at himself for what he was about to do, but simultaneously unable to stop himself.

"Rhett, wake up," he said, this time his voice louder and more stern.

"Fuck."

Rhett flailed, his body flying backward, leaving Cole bereft and cold. Rhett took the sheets with him, tangling his legs in the soft cotton and tumbling onto the floor with a thud. Cole adjusted his cock and crawled over to the edge of the bed, looking down at Rhett.

"Are you okay?"

Rhett pulled the sheet free of his legs and used it to cover his face. "I'm so embarrassed, oh, my God."

"Why?" Cole reached down and gripped the sheet, trying to pull it away from Rhett's face.

Rhett groaned and rolled to face the wall. He was wrapped up in the sheet and the curve of his ass came into Cole's view, thankfully covered by his bright blue briefs and not bare, but what an ass it was.

"Babe," Cole tried.

"Stoooop," Rhett whined, fighting the sheet away from his face and narrowing his eyes at Cole. "I'll just sleep down here until we go home."

Cole laughed, "Why on earth would you do that?"

"It's a giant bed!" Rhett gestured wildly, forcing himself onto his feet, the sheet wrapped around his legs and pooling around his ankles.

His cock was hard.

Cole threw an arm across his eyes, but it was too late. The outline of Rhett's cock, smashed into those tight briefs, was seared in his memory. He'd wank over it for the rest of his life, starting right now.

"I'm going to shower," he rushed the words out, crawling out of the other side of the bed and locking himself in the bathroom.

He cranked the hot water and stepped under the spray, jerking his cock until he came against the wall of the shower. He groaned, watching the evidence of his orgasm slide down the tile. His cock didn't waver, still thick and hard even after his orgasm. Cole reached for the taps, turning the water cold. He shivered, but stayed until his erection abated.

Once he was confident his cock was done, he turned the warm water higher and finished his shower, shampooing his hair then washing and rinsing all the other necessary parts of a man that required attention. He turned off the taps and stepped onto the bathmat, swiping a hand across the fogged mirror. He scratched his fingernails into his two day scruff, hoping that Kristen wasn't going to cause a scene if he didn't shave. Being able to release even that one small responsibility was liberating.

Cole wrapped a towel around his waist and exited the bathroom, only to find the hotel room empty. The sliding glass door to the beach was open and Cole stepped outside. The morning light was bright and it was warm, as it always was in Tahiti, but not hot enough to cause him to sweat yet.

Rhett was in the ocean, not deep, just far enough that the waves lapped at his knees. He was still, a figure on the horizon that Cole somehow could already describe in details he had no right knowing. He closed his eyes, pictured himself wading into the water and coming behind Rhett, wrapping his arms around and turning him, pressing their lips together and kissing him until they couldn't breathe.

The fantasy was a vivid one, down to the sound and the feeling of their teeth clacking together as they nipped at each other's lips and tongues. He exhaled a rough breath, mentally turning Rhett's sleepy touches from earlier into purposeful movements that stripped Cole of his clothes.

"Are you done in the bathroom?"

He opened his eyes and Rhett was in front of him, skin damp with salt water.

"Obviously," Cole rasped, trying to reconcile real Rhett with this fantasy he couldn't shake.

Rhett nodded then dipped his head, walking past him and straight through the room into the bathroom. Cole took the icy reception for what it was, returning to the room behind Rhett and dressing quickly. He scribbled out a note saying he'd be back before lunch, then slipped out of the room.

He didn't have a plan, but he knew putting space between them was necessary. Cole found himself in one of the small hotel restaurants where he ordered a coffee and croissant. He scrolled through the news on his phone, checking in with his operations manager back at the vineyard and catching up with a handful of other missed emails that needed attention.

"Where is that boyfriend of yours?"

A piercing voice from behind caused him to wince. He bit his tongue and forced a smile. "Good morning, Nan."

"That wasn't an answer." She leaned against the chair across from him without sitting in it, which Cole was thankful for.

"He's in our room," Cole answered curtly.

"You know, Cole, I was talking with your grandfather last night and we both agreed that it was so absurd that you had a boyfriend and no one knew about it."

"I respectfully disagree, Nan. I'm a busy man, running Mallory. I didn't want anyone to get excited at the prospect of me settling down with anyone until I knew it was serious." For the most part, that entire statement was true. Things with Rhett were serious, but more like seriously stressful and seriously fucked up.

"Have you talked with your sister about the operations at the vineyard?"

Cole licked the front of his teeth and clenched his jaw. "She has no interest in the vineyard, Nan."

"That's a shame."

Cole's stomach twisted. "Why?"

His grandmother gave a sort of careless looking half-shrug perfected by those who were far too close to the end of their days to extend any common courtesy to those around them.

"Will we be seeing your boyfriend, what's his name, Royce, at the wedding tonight?"

Cole's mouth twitched.

"His name is Rhett, and of course he'll be at the wedding. He's my date."

"Very well then, Cole." His grandmother flicked her hand in lieu of saying goodbye and left him alone, her heels clicking through the restaurant and back to the lobby.

Cole took a drink of his coffee, which was nearly cold now, and returned his attention to his phone in time to see a text come in from his sister.

Kristen: I didn't know you were fucking the towel boy.

Me: Why do you insist on calling him that?
Kristen: Well, he is.
Me: ????
Kristen: Doesn't his family rent towels? Isn't that what you said at lunch?
Me: God, you're daft. They're a linen rental company. Tablecloths and shit. For weddings. Like the one you're about to have tonight that I assume will have tablecloths and napkins, right?
Kristen: You're annoyingly literal.
Me: You're annoyingly bitchy. Why are you even texting me? Shouldn't you be drinking champagne and getting your hair done?
Kristen: I am doing all of those things, brother dear. Sandy found this sparkling rosé and it's so good. Can you make rosé at home?
Me: It's literally not that easy.
Kristen: You should look into it. Rosé is all the rage.
Me: I will, Kris.
Me: Go hang out with your friends. I'll see you tonight.
Kristen: It's literally my weekend, Cole, you don't get to tell me what to do.
Me: Be that as it may, I'm done talking to you. I had a terrible conversation with Nan and I just want to drink my coffee.
Kristen: What did she want????
Me: No one knows. Don't worry about it. Enjoy your day.
Me: You only get married for the first time once.
Kristen: Fuck you.

His phone rang, Ryan's face lighting up the screen and interrupting whatever colorful emojis Kristen was most assuredly about to send him. Cole sighed, regretting that he'd even taken his phone out of his suitcase before he left Rhett in the bathroom earlier.

He accepted the call.

"Hey."

"Hey there, bestie," Ryan said, his voice teasing and lyrical.

"How are things at home?"

"Fuck home," Ryan laughed, "How are things in paradise?"

"Everything is great," Cole half-lied, making a mental note that lying hadn't ever come as easy as it had the past week.

"You and my baby brother having fun?" Ryan's voice had a slight edge to it.

"He's three minutes younger than you," Cole remarked.

"Don't dodge the question."

"We've been having a nice time," Cole told the truth. "It's nice being here with him."

Ryan made some sort of partially agreeable noise. "I wish you would have told me."

"I didn't want things to be weird, like if things with him didn't work out."

"Will it be weird if things *do* work out?" Ryan asked.

"Things *are* working out, dude."

"Right, yeah. I mean that's good."

"Are you sure?" Cole asked, really hoping that this whole plan he and Rhett had hatched wouldn't fuck up either of their relationships with Ryan.

"I am," Ryan promised. "It's just weird. Anyway, what are you doing? I didn't interrupt anything?"

Cole scoffed. "You interrupted me trying to drink my coffee in peace. I love you, but I regret turning my phone on so I'm hanging up now. I'll talk to you when we're home."

Cole hung up his phone then turned it to silent and flipped it face down on the table. He didn't want to talk with anyone else today if they weren't Rhett and that terrified him.

Chapter Sixteen
RHETT

❦

Somehow, Rhett hadn't expected Cole to vanish while he showered. He read the note Cole left, promising to return by lunch. Rhett flipped it over and scrawled something similar on the other side of the page. He wasn't a kid who needed his hand held and he had things he wanted to do while he was here.

He went to his suitcase and fished out his camera, a Nikon that he'd saved up forever for. His boss, Macy, had given him a crash course in photography after he'd bought it and the rest he learned through a combination of watching her and experimenting.

Rhett skipped breakfast, he wasn't entirely hungry after his morning of mortification, and left the hotel. He walked along the beach, taking photos of things that interested him. White sand clinging to his feet. A low hanging palm frond. Anonymous footprints. His toes digging into the sand.

The harder Rhett tried to not think about earlier, the more he inevitably thought about it. About waking up next to Cole and those three nanoseconds where he'd forgotten this was pretend, that he wasn't supposed to be snuggled up next to Cole using him for a pillow and basically humping his leg.

He'd escaped to the water when Cole scrambled into the

shower to get away from him. Rhett frowned and took a picture of a single palm tree and endless blue sky. The hotel room had felt too small with both of them in it, and Rhett went outside, needing to feel something on his skin that wasn't Cole.

He lowered his camera and sighed. It hadn't worked at all. Rhett could still feel the way Cole's skin had been warm against his. The way his body wasn't hard or soft, but was instead the sort of perfection Rhett thought he'd only been dreaming about.

Arriving at the same market he'd been to the day before, Rhett took his time again, strolling through, eyeing the colorful fabrics. His heart tightened when he saw a particularly colorful pot that he could put Lucy in. He snapped a picture of it, sure it would never survive in his suitcase, and left it behind.

Rhett came to the end of the street market and stopped. Tahiti wasn't the same without Cole and his musical laugh, without his perfect sort of company that was neither too chatty nor too quiet. Cole had made Tahiti beautiful. He'd loved experiencing things with Cole and without him, Rhett's surroundings diminished from being paradise to being a too-hot beach too far from home.

He returned to the empty hotel room and tucked his camera away. He dug his e-reader out and curled up in one of the chairs to read. It was nearly lunch and Cole was due to return any minute. Rhett tried to focus on his book, but ended up staring at the words, listening for the door to open. He suddenly felt like a kid with a crush, trying too hard to look relaxed and ultimately giving themselves away with how not relaxed they really were.

He set his e-reader aside and, though it was too early to dress for the wedding, decided that another shower might be prudent. He'd walked along the sandy beaches slathered in sunscreen that smelled of coconut and he'd probably sweated too much.

He refused to touch himself this time, despite the urge that thrummed in his blood and lived under his skin—to come with Cole's face in his mind and his name on his lips. He couldn't do that after this morning. Instead he ignored his dick, giving it a perfunctory wash before scrubbing himself clean. Not wanting to linger in the spray, lest he give into the urge to think of dangerous things, he stepped out and wrapped a towel around his waist.

He shaved, not that he really needed to. His facial hair grew thick, but slowly. Ryan joked with him that it took him three days to grow a five o'clock shadow. Rhett always thought he was just jealous because it took Ryan three hours to grow one.

He should call Ryan, he thought as he cleaned the last of the shaving cream off his face. Or Penny. Just so he could talk to someone who wasn't Cole. Someone he could actually think around.

The bathroom door swung open and Rhett leaped back, a startled squeak spilling out of his lips even as his brain registered that it was just Cole. After he'd calmed, he smiled and laughed, because it was funny, but he was also ridiculously happy to see Cole.

"Hi. Holy crap, you scared me."

Cole's smile wasn't as bright and Rhett wondered how uncomfortable he'd made him that morning. He felt as if the life were draining out of him.

"Um. About this morning. I'm sorry, Cole. I swear I didn't mean to use you for a human body pillow. I didn't mean to make you uncomfortable." Rhett felt as if he were about to start babbling. He gripped his towel, insuring it wouldn't slide off and embarrass himself even more.

"It's fine, Rhett. I promise." Cole moved toward him and he skirted away slightly, trying to angle himself to slip past Cole.

"Okay. Um. I should get dressed."

"Rhett, wait."

Whenever Cole said his name, Rhett couldn't breathe. He wanted Cole to say his name over and over again. His name was suddenly more than a name. When Cole said it, it became a spell that only worked for Cole. Rhett stopped moving.

Cole reached for his face, cupped his cheek. His thumb stroked over a patch of Rhett's skin. Tender. Electric. The touch was so many things. Cole pulled his hand away far too soon and smiled at Rhett, showing him his thumb.

"You had some shaving cream."

An illusion. Like everything else.

"Thanks." Rhett said, his voice sounding too tight, too thin. He found himself unable to fake happiness in that moment. He dropped his gaze and slid away from Cole. "We'll be late."

"Right. Yeah. Be right out."

While Cole showered, again, Rhett did his best not to think of him naked while he slid into the suit Cole had helped him pick out for the wedding. Rhett thought the suspenders made him look a little too nerdy, but Cole had grinned at him and proclaimed there to be no such thing as too nerdy. Rhett slipped his tie on and tightened it as Cole came out of the bathroom, freshly showered and already dressed in his suit.

He was gorgeous. Rhett wasn't sure that he'd ever seen Cole Mallory look so good or so dressed up. The suit fit him perfectly, accentuating the length of his limbs, his broad shoulders, and his trim waist. Cole fastened the button of his jacket and tugged at the sleeves.

"You look fantastic," Cole said, his gaze raking over Rhett slowly, heating every inch of him from across the room.

Rhett suddenly wished he'd jacked off in the shower. "So do you."

Then they said nothing. Until Cole started to laugh. His fingers fluttered at his hairline before he pulled them away and shoved them in his pockets instead of messing his hair. "We need this to not be awkward, Rhett."

Rhett nodded. "I know."

"How do we make this not awkward? Things haven't been weird until now."

Rhett shrugged a shoulder and tore his gaze away. He reached for his jacket to find Cole suddenly in front of him. Close enough to smell his cologne, to feel the heat radiate off him, to almost feel the air puff out of his mouth as Cole's hand reached for his.

"Look at me, Rhett."

He couldn't possibly do anything but.

Rhett looked at Cole, who was both too sincere and too intense. "Tell me what to do to fix this."

Rhett exhaled. His breath shaking, his whole body vibrating from the emotional ferocity of the moment. He looked at Cole, and blinked, and tried not to smile.

"Hump my leg. It's only fair."

Cole's eyes widened, then he laughed and pulled Rhett into him, hugging him tight, laughing into the curve of his neck, his arms winding around Rhett. Their bodies shook as they laughed, releasing all the pent up tension of the morning. When they finally composed themselves, Cole released Rhett and dashed a tear out of his eye. "That was perfect."

Cole beamed as Rhett slid his arms into his jacket.

He buttoned it and took Cole's hand automatically. "Lead the way."

"I feel as if I should warn you."

Rhett laughed. "I promise to keep my eyes out for crabs. I won't be scared so easily a second time."

Cole chuckled, but squeezed Rhett's hand. "My grandmother is old, cranky, and in a mood. She asked about you this morning."

"That doesn't sound so bad."

"She wanted to know why we weren't together. She can't even get your name right, but expects you to live in my pocket." Rhett could hear Cole's voice tighten as he got more and more heated. "I hate putting you through all of this, Rhett. I'm asking a lot."

"You're not asking anything that I didn't agree to do."

"My sister was horrible to you." Cole grimaced and it looked as though he was going to continue, but Rhett stopped him.

"She's always horrible, Cole. She's horrible to everyone. I'd be worried if she were nice to me, to be honest."

"You didn't agree to take abuse from my family."

Rhett suppressed a laugh. "That's what happens when you get married, Cole. You sign up for better or worse. It's fine. I promise."

"But, Rhett," he started to say but Rhett shushed him.

"Stop," he said, pulling them to a stop and stepping in front of

Cole, their fingers still linked. He let go and reached for Cole's face, learning that it was soft, with a bit of stubble along his jaw. "Stop. It's okay."

"But they're going to expect things from us. From you. A certain level of...you know..."

Rhett smiled, his thumb stroking a trail across Cole's perfect cheekbone. "Then let's give them what they want."

Rhett leaned closer, tasting Cole's breath on his skin. Cole trembled, or maybe it was himself, he couldn't tell. The only thing he was sure about in that moment was the feel of Cole's lips as they finally touched his own. Tender and soft, tentative at first, then more insistent. Long and slow, the moment stretched out until it was so big Rhett felt as if time could stop and he could live right there, like this.

Rhett pulled away and blinked at Cole, then reluctantly pulled his hand away from Cole's face. "We're going to be late." Cole nodded and Rhett gave his hand a squeeze.

"It's going to be fine, I promise." Rhett said, vowing to do his best today to make sure he kept that promise. He wouldn't let Cole down.

Chapter Seventeen
COLE

Kristen and Edward were married now. Cole assumed as much because he was at the reception with Rhett, holding Rhett's hand, sitting next to him, drinking champagne. Their shoulders were touching and Cole could still taste Rhett on his lips.

"I'd expect to see you two out there dancing," his mother said, dropping down heavily into an empty chair at their table. Rhett tipped his half-empty champagne glass in her direction.

"Pacing ourselves, Mother," Cole answered. Rhett squeezed his hand in solidarity.

"The evening is nearly over," she countered, "Kristen has already cut the cake and now that the sun has set, she won't like any of the pictures because they'll come out too dark."

"Sounds like something she would say," Cole laughed.

"Nighttime photography is really hard," Rhett interjected. "You have to know how to frame things without getting unnecessary shadows and you need to have a good eye for finding the light you need. You can't use a flash because everything washes out."

Cole's mother raised an eyebrow in Rhett's direction. "How do you know all that?"

The rest of her question was unspoken, but Cole heard it in his head, bouncing around in his sister's voice. *How do you know all that? Aren't you just the towel boy?* Cole despised that nickname. It was one his sister had directed at Ryan for years. Her dependence on the family wealth made her think she was far above anyone who was working class and it made Cole sick.

"I adore photography," Rhett answered gracefully. "I took classes in college and it's something I've continued to dabble in. I was out taking pictures earlier today, actually. The island is beautiful."

"I suppose," Cole's mother agreed, dismissing Rhett's answer entirely. "Anyway, have you stopped to say hello to your grandparents?"

"I've been trying to avoid them," Cole admitted. He reached for his champagne flute and finished it in one swallow.

"That's a poor play on your part, Cole." Constance stood and smoothed the fluttery purple organza fabric in her skirt. "Have a good rest of the evening, boys."

She stepped away from the table, leaving them again in peace.

"Should we go say hello?" Rhett asked, resting his head on Cole's shoulder.

"It's like the godfather," he sighed. "This whole kiss the ring bullshit."

"Except kissing a ring would be a lot easier than orchestrating a fake relationship," Rhett countered with a laugh.

Cole pushed back his chair and stood, pulling Rhett with him. "That's a terrible thing for my future fake husband to say. Come on then, let's get it over with."

Cole guided Rhett through the reception, skirting the edges of the dance floor. It was practically empty now, a few couples managing some jerky dance moves to the beat of whatever popular dance song the DJ was playing. The only people left were mostly family. Kristen and her friends gathered near the door as she and Edward made their exit.

"Lovely wedding, Nan," Cole remarked, coming to a stop

beside his grandmother's chair. She looked up at him with a tight smile.

"A bit gaudy for my taste."

Getting married in Tahiti itself was gaudy, Cole thought, but he didn't vocalize it.

"What did you think?" she asked, directing her attention to Rhett.

"Oh, I thought it was very fitting," he answered, slipping an arm around Cole's waist. "And it definitely had its romantic moments."

Cole swallowed and reached behind him, sliding his palm across the top of Rhett's hand. His skin was so warm.

"In my day, we got married in churches," Cole's grandfather piped up.

"Well, in your day, women didn't get to wear pants. Things have changed," Cole teased.

His grandfather snorted and nodded.

"Anyway," Rhett said with a smile, "we just wanted to come say hello. Cole has promised me a dance and I intend to collect on it before the DJ packs up."

"A dance," Cole said, even though he'd agreed to no such thing. Being that close to Rhett while people watched was a terrible plan for both of them.

"Very well," Cole's grandmother said with a nod, as though giving them permission. "I'm ready to turn in, George."

She turned to her husband and he exhaled loudly before helping her up from the table. Cole watched them until they left and turned to Rhett, relieved.

"Did you want to take off?" Cole asked, grateful the pressure was gone.

"No," Rhett scoffed, grabbing for Cole's hand. "You owe me a dance."

"We don't need to," Cole waved a hand behind him toward the door. "They're gone."

"You know this farce doesn't end just because your family isn't around, right?" Rhett asked, stopping on the dance floor and pulling Cole against his chest. "It needs to be convincing, like you said. Everyone thinks we've been seeing each other for months. Dancing at a wedding is expected."

Rhett slid his hands around Cole's waist and held him close. Cole could feel Rhett's fingertips against his hips, the heat of his touch igniting his skin even through the fabric of his shirt. Reluctantly, Cole wrapped his arms around Rhett, palms flat against his back.

"I love this song," Rhett murmured, leaning even closer and resting his head against Cole's shoulder. Reflexively, Cole smoothed his hands up Rhett's back and held their bodies tight against each other.

Cole hummed the opening bars of "Unforgettable", his nose buried in Rhett's hair. He was thankful his dick hadn't popped up due to the forced proximity of their lower halves, but he found other feelings to be far more prominent than arousal.

His heart, for example, twisted and expanded, stuttered and skipped, all depending on what he thought about. It slammed against his ribs, aching when he reminded himself it wasn't real.

Rhett's heart was racing, its beat so violent and staccato Cole could feel it against his own. He was suddenly too hot, too tense, his clothes too constraining. He reached between them and fumbled for his bow tie, desperate to alleviate some of the pressure around his neck so he could breathe.

Rhett pulled back slightly, his skin bright like a star under the glow of the string lights that zig-zagged over the top of the dance floor. His eyes were somehow hazy, yet focused at the same time. He pulled his hands away from Cole's waist and he was mournful of the loss until Rhett reached between them, stilling his hand against the silk of the tie.

"Let me help you," he whispered, gripping the loose end of Cole's tie and pulling the bow apart. The fabric unfolded and then Rhett's fingers were at the top button of his shirt, popping it loose before sliding down to the next. He undid that button as well, placing his hands against Cole's chest in a way that allowed his fingertips to glide across the naked V of Cole's chest.

"Rhett," Cole exhaled his name like a prayer.

"Sssh." Rhett shook his head and didn't move his hands, still gripping the collar of Cole's shirt between his fingers. He looked up at Cole, their faces so close, mouths *so* close.

They swayed together on the dance floor, and Cole didn't even realize the music had stopped until Rhett looked over his shoulder toward the DJ booth.

"Play that one again," he said, turning his face back to Cole. "It's my favorite."

The piano introduction to "Unforgettable" started up again and Rhett smiled up at him dreamily. Cole was losing willpower by the minute, unable to deny that there was something sparking between them that was far beyond playing a role. They'd been dancing around each other for the past three days, pretending they didn't want to wake up in each other's arms, treating this thing between them like a show.

Cole closed his eyes, mentally replaying the kiss they'd shared before the wedding. The hot warmth of Rhett's mouth, the soft dance of his fingers, the smoothness of his lips.

"And forevermore, that's how you'll stay," Rhett whispered along to the song and Cole opened his eyes, daring a look at the man in his arms.

The smart, and talented, and handsome man in his arms.

Rhett's fingers were still at his collar and Cole felt them dip underneath the fabric, sliding slowly, almost cautiously up his throat. Rhett traced a path of fire until he reached Cole's chin, dragging his way up the arch of his jaw before pushing his fingers into his hair.

How was Rhett closer now? When did they get closer? Cole inhaled a sharp breath, not even sure he'd taken one in the past five minutes.

"Rhett," he tried to say again, his voice no more than a harsh whisper. He didn't even know what he wanted to say, but the need to let Rhett know he was here and in the moment seemed imperative.

"Cole," Rhett answered back, his thumbs stroking across Cole's cheeks.

God, he looked beautiful under these lights.

Rhett pulled Cole's face toward him, less than an inch, and their lips touched. The kiss wasn't like the one from earlier; this one was calmer, more measured. Rhett took command of him, his tongue sliding across the seam of Cole's lips until they parted. He licked his way into Cole's mouth, pulling back before coming close again, each kiss longer and more passionate than the last.

Rhett's hands held Cole's face steady while he took what he wanted, and Cole gripped Rhett's shoulders, making sure he didn't stop. Cole kissed him back, angling his head and slanting his mouth, his tongue dueling with Rhett's for purchase in the space between their mouths.

Cole's cock was hard now, pressing against Rhett's thigh, against Rhett's own erection, but it didn't stop either of them. Rhett kept kissing him and Cole kept sliding his feet, leading the dance.

He didn't know how much time had passed, but when they finally separated, the room was bright and the music was over. Cole rested his forehead against Rhett's and raised his hands to cup Rhett's neck.

The island air smelled like water and flowers, but in that moment all Cole smelled was the lingering hint of Rhett's cologne mixed with sweat and the sweet champagne on his breath. He wasn't certain, but he had a fleeting thought that this moment here, right now, was what falling in love was like.

"I don't want to do this anymore," Rhett whispered.

"What?" Cole croaked, his perfectly fabricated memory cracking around him in real time.

"I don't want to pretend I don't want you," Rhett said, nipping at Cole's lower lip with his teeth.

Cole sighed and kissed Rhett back, more aggressive than before, more confident, more *ready*. He pulled away, breathing heavily and dragging his mouth across Rhett's swollen lips.

"Then don't."

Chapter Eighteen
RHETT

Sometime between the awkward tour of his apartment and the dance floor at a wedding in Tahiti, his fake relationship with Cole had brewed a very real attraction. He wasn't supposed to want Cole the way he needed him. The architecture of his face shouldn't have been captivating. Cole's scent shouldn't have been addicting. Somehow it was. Somehow every part of Rhett wanted to know every part of Cole.

The lie he'd been telling himself had slowly unraveled and the kiss before the wedding had crushed it completely. Cole's words tugged at Rhett's cock.

"Then don't."

A green light. Permission to want. Permission to stop lying to himself, to both of them. Rhett crashed their mouths together again, tasting Cole, breathing him in, listening to the broken moan that stuttered out of himself as he dragged their mouths apart.

Rhett laced their fingers together and prayed that Cole wouldn't change his mind before they got back to their room. He feared that this moment, this perfect moment, was a bubble, and that any time wasted would pop it. He might only have a finite number of minutes, and if he did, he wanted to spend them in Cole's arms—tasting his skin, drowning in his heady gaze.

He tugged Cole toward the exit and past the crew who had come to clean up. Rhett slowed down a little when they hit the beach. It wasn't far to their room and the sun had set hours ago. The moon was bright and full and Rhett could still hear "Unforgettable" playing on loop in his mind.

The moment between them swelled when they walked into their room. They hadn't spoken since the dance floor and Rhett wasn't sure how much was left to say. He let Cole pull him close. He shuddered when Cole kissed him below his ear, instinctively finding the spot that made Rhett weak in the knees.

He shoved his fingers in Cole's hair, loving that it was as soft as he imagined it to be, and pulled Cole's mouth to his. Kissing Cole had become his new favorite thing. His mouth was hot and sweet and currently tasted like champagne, but better. He let his hands slide down Cole's chest. First tugging the loose tie off him and tossing it aside, then finding the buttons and continuing to undo them, one by one, as Cole moaned in his mouth and did his own explorations of Rhett's body with his hands.

Cole tugged Rhett's shirt free of his pants while Rhett shoved Cole's shirt off his shoulders.

"Naked," Rhett groaned, breaking the kiss and reaching for the button on Cole's pants. "We need to be way more naked."

Cole stole a kiss, his eyes fluttering closed, the moment tender on Rhett's lips and warm in his heart. Then Cole pulled away and let Rhett undo his pants while he toed out of his shoes. They undressed in a flurry of activity. Cole shoving his pants down and pulling them off while Rhett hurried to unbutton his shirt as he kicked his shoes off.

Rhett paused when they were fully naked to take in the sight of Cole bathed in moonlight, his cock hard, standing proud against his stomach. His swollen lips were parted, and he breathed Rhett's name in a reverent sort of way that made Rhett need to kiss him again.

He pulled Cole close to him, their cocks bumping together between their bodies. He wrapped his arms around Cole and kissed him, kissed him with every ounce of passion he felt for him. He turned Cole so his back was to the bed.

Their descent to the mattress was slow, a dance of limbs and balance. Their landing was soft and Rhett lay on top, Cole's hands kneading the meat of his ass. Rhett broke away from Cole's mouth and kissed his jaw, his neck, his clavicle, peppering soft kisses up the slope.

"Rhett. Fuck," Cole said when Rhett flicked a nipple with his tongue.

"Mmhm," Rhett agreed as he moved down the bed, down Cole, doing his best to kiss every inch of skin between his mouth and his cock. He smoothed his hands down Cole's body and gazed up at him. Cole had propped himself up on his elbows to watch Rhett.

He leaned forward. Cole's cock twitched and Rhett smiled, then stuck his tongue out and licked a long, wet line from root to tip, drawing a broken curse out of Cole's mouth as he flopped back onto the bed. He threw his arm over his face, then seemingly thought better of it because he pulled it away and stared down at Rhett again.

He hadn't let himself imagine having Cole like this, but now that the moment was here, Rhett wouldn't waste it. He took the head of Cole's cock in his mouth, swirled his tongue around it, then took more into his mouth. Cole's hand sank into Rhett's hair, holding firmly, but not tight. A reminder that he was there, that he needed this as much as Rhett did. That he wanted it with the same sort of single-minded intensity.

Cole tasted like skin, like skin and salt and Cole. Like something he could taste every day and never get tired of. Rhett took him deeper, deeper again, until his nose was pressed into his thatch of dark pubic hair and Cole was swearing, arching off the bed.

Rhett pulled off; needing air, he wrapped his hand around

Cole's cock and laved his balls with his tongue. Taking one gently into his mouth, he rolled his tongue around it.

"Holy fuck, Rhett." Cole's voice raised in pitch slightly. "Oh, my God," he proclaimed when Rhett shoved his legs apart, giving him better access to all of Cole.

Rhett smiled and kissed the crease of Cole's thigh. Once. Twice. He looked up at Cole when he kissed him a third time, mapping the contours of Cole's face. Memorizing the angles of his body, the feel of his skin, everything he never wanted to forget.

"Kiss me." Cole licked his lips. "Please."

Rhett climbed up the bed, straddling him. He grabbed his face and ghosted his lips across Cole's. "Anything," Rhett promised before kissing him. "I could lie here all night and do nothing but kiss you," he admitted. He wanted to, but he wouldn't and they both knew it.

He kissed Cole again, moaning into his mouth, writhing his hips, pushing their erections together, grinding, sliding, needing friction and heat. Needing Cole.

"I want you," he breathed against Cole's neck, enjoying the way Cole kissed at his neck, half tender, half ferocious with nips and bites mixed in with the softest of caresses.

"You have me." Cole slammed their mouths together. Their teeth clacked, making the moment theirs in an imperfect sort of way.

Rhett scrambled off the bed and dug in his suitcase, getting the condoms and the lube he'd brought. Just in case. Maybe he'd always known this would happen. Maybe he'd hoped it right from the beginning. He returned to Cole, who looked at the supplies, but stayed silent despite his obvious amusement.

"Can I?" Rhett asked, dropping the condoms on the bed, but keeping the lube.

"Please," Cole whispered.

Rhett squeezed lube on a couple of his fingers and Cole spread his legs, allowing Rhett to reach between them and press his slick fingers against his ass. He circled the rim, his breath trembling, his body vibrating with need and fear. With desire and terror. He needed Cole so bad every bone in his body ached with it, and when this was over, how would anyone else compare?

Rhett didn't care. He made himself not care. He wanted to know what it was like. To touch him, to hold him. To kiss him and want him without restraint. Without anything hanging over their head. No grandparents looming, no family to put on a show for. This moment was theirs. No matter what happened down the road, Rhett wanted this moment.

He eased his fingers inside Cole slowly, one at first, then two, moving in and out, loosening him up. Cole pressed his eyes shut, held fistfuls of blanket and panted, moving to fuck himself on Rhett's fingers.

"More."

Rhett pulled his fingers out of Cole and grabbed a condom. He unrolled it down his cock, coated it with lube, then moved into position. With Cole's legs around his waist, Rhett pressed into him, moving slowly, savoring the way Cole's body opened to accommodate him.

Rhett's entire body shook and he kissed Cole, burying himself as deep into him as he could, his hips gliding and snapping, thrusting himself into Cole as his hands dug into Rhett's back. Fingers biting his skin, legs constricting around him, heels digging into Rhett's ass.

He pulled back and looked at Cole, held his gaze and slowed his pace, his own orgasm nearing too soon. He slowed until the heat left his spine, until the tug in his balls became less insistent.

"Cole," Rhett started speaking before he was entirely sure of what he was going to say. He gripped Cole's shoulders and plunged deeper, slamming into him as hard as he could. He dropped his head and squeezed his eyes shut and did it again. Cole clung to him, called out for him.

"Rhett, fuck. Rhett. Holy shit."

"God, you feel so good," Rhett admitted. "Fuck, you feel amazing, babe. Oh, my God."

"Rhett. Let me fuck you. Please, Rhett." Cole arched his back, his fingers digging into Rhett's sides. "Want to feel you, too."

Rhett stilled, then draped himself over Cole, pressing their chests together, he grabbed Cole's face and kissed him, long and deep, taking his time, luxuriating in the moment, drawing every kiss out as long as he could to make up for all the times he'd wanted to kiss Cole and didn't. Couldn't. All the times since the afternoon at the vineyard when he'd been too drunk to stop himself and just drunk enough to see what an amazing person Cole was.

Rhett slid out of Cole, but kept kissing him. Cole's arms wrapped around Rhett and in a blur of movement, Rhett was suddenly on the bottom, staring up at Cole with his heart in his chest, feeling naked beyond having no clothes.

"Rhett," Cole said.

"Anything," Rhett answered. Tonight, and maybe for longer, the answer to whatever Cole wanted from him would be anything.

He moaned when Cole reached down and rolled the condom off of his cock and tossed it aside. He wrapped a hand around Rhett's dick and the look he gave him made him melt.

"Anything is a dangerous word."

Rhett wanted to respond, but couldn't because no matter the danger, no matter the potential outcome, he wanted this. And he wanted this more than he feared it.

"Anything," he repeated, imploring Cole to believe him.

Chapter Nineteen
COLE

❦

Cole ached from use and want. He gripped Rhett's ass cheeks in his hands, spreading him apart and swiping his tongue up from his hole to his balls. Rhett jerked and Cole held him tighter, licking tight swirls around Rhett's ass, using spit to lube him up. He eased a finger inside, pressing his tongue against the tight seal Rhett's body formed around his knuckle.

"Please," Rhett begged.

"I don't think I want to take my time with you after all," Cole told him. He unrolled a condom down his length and aligned his cock with Rhett's entrance. He grabbed the lube and slicked his cock and Rhett's crack, using the head of his dick to spread the lube around.

"You better not," Rhett rasped.

Cole pushed inside, his cock stretching Rhett until he whimpered beneath him. He stilled. "Too much?"

Rhett bore down, his muscles tightening and then giving way and letting Cole deeper.

"Jesus," Cole breathed out. He bottomed out and stayed, flexing his fingers against Rhett's waist.

This was better than he'd imagined. If every shower wank

where he'd thought about Rhett had happened at the same time, it wouldn't have felt this good. His body trembled and his cock pulsed. He was ready to come, but he wasn't anywhere close to being ready for this to end.

Rhett was babbling promises of anything, and forever, and always, and Cole didn't know if he meant it, but he hoped he did. He'd been fantasizing about a future with Rhett that he was desperate to fully realize and with Rhett beneath him, it seemed possible.

"You said you wouldn't hold back," Rhett grunted, the muscles of his channel gripping Cole's cock.

He growled and grabbed Rhett, flipping him onto his stomach and hoisting him onto his knees. He buried himself inside of Rhett, snaking an arm around his chest and holding him up, pressing their bodies together. He sank his teeth into Rhett's neck and pounded him from behind, hips bucking feverishly.

Sweat dripped into his eyes and he used Rhett's hair to wipe his face. He reached around and fisted Rhett's cock.

"Is this real?"

Heat flamed up Cole's spine and he cried out Rhett's name, hips snapping forward, balls emptying themselves into the condom.

"Oh, fuck," Rhett panted.

Cole's hand was warm, slick with Rhett's cum, and he continued to pump his fist around Rhett's dick. He pulled back, his own cock sliding free of Rhett's hole. He patted the gaping and tender flesh with a sweaty hand and Rhett shook violently in his arms, angling his head to the side to search out Cole's mouth.

Cole kissed him back, their teeth again smashing together, nipping at each other's flesh, then Rhett was gone, collapsed on the bed beneath him with a happy sigh. His back was slick with sweat and splotchy red. Cole traced the shapes with his finger, adding the kaleidoscope blush of Rhett's body to the secrets about his boyfriend that he'd never share.

Rhett wasn't his boyfriend though. Cole lowered himself to the sheets, breathing heavily and feeling somehow sated and forlorn at the same time. He'd just ejaculated what felt like his entire soul and it was for what? A man who wasn't really his?

He removed the condom and tied it off, tossing it onto the floor. Rhett shimmied across the bed, raking his short nails across Cole's chest affectionately. Cole stilled his hand.

"I know we just did it, but when can we do it again?" he asked with a tired smile.

"Again?" Cole questioned, turning to face Rhett.

"I told you I didn't want to pretend. I mean *that* wasn't pretend. Was it?"

"It wasn't pretend," Cole agreed, releasing Rhett's hand. Rhett flexed his fingers against Cole's chest and tickled them lightly across his skin.

"So, again then?" Rhett's hand snaked down his chest toward his cock.

"I don't know, Rhett."

"What's not to know?"

"Fucking each other puts this whole thing in jeopardy," Cole reminded him.

Rhett twisted his face into a scornful look. "It definitely does no such thing. We're supposed to be fucking anyway. That's what couples do. If anything, this adds to our credibility." He traced a finger down Cole's shaft, making him shudder. "You'll react to me differently now when I'm around."

Rhett rolled his head on the pillow and licked the shell of Cole's ear. "Because you'll know what it feels like when I'm inside of you."

"Jesus," Cole exhaled.

"Just me."

Cole chuckled. "So is this friends with benefits then?"

Rhett propped himself up on his elbow and looked down at Cole. "Do you want to be my friend?"

"We've been friends," Cole reminded him.

"This doesn't seem very friendly."

"This seems far *too* friendly."

Rhett laughed and dropped onto his back, lacing his fingers together behind his head and sighing happily.

"I don't want to just be your friend, Cole."

Cole swallowed thickly, his heart trying to make an escape out of his throat. "Alright."

"You're not the most romantic one, are you?"

Cole moved quickly, covering Rhett's body with his own and slanting their mouths together in a gentle kiss. "Just wait until I propose to you."

"It doesn't count if I told you how I want you to do it, and besides, this may be real, but that definitely wouldn't be."

"Why not?" Cole asked, brows furrowed.

"We've been fake dating. Now we're barely real dating. How could a proposal in three months be real?"

"You think that's what's going to happen between now and Christmas?" Cole teased. "We're just going to fake date, but it'll be a little less fake than before tonight?"

"Basically," Rhett agreed.

"Ye of little faith." Cole jumped off the bed, padding naked into the bathroom. He began a mental checklist of all the things he planned to do with Rhett between now and Christmas just to make sure he knew that Cole was all in.

He turned on the shower and waited for the water to warm. Rhett appeared in the doorway and approached him, wrapping his arms around Cole's waist and flattening his cheek against his shoulder blade.

"Why can't we real date with a fake proposal?" Rhett propositioned, peeking around Cole's side and searching out his eyes in the mirror.

"Do you think that would work?" He moved toward the shower, taking Rhett with him.

"It has as much a chance of working as it did when it was one-hundred percent fake."

Cole handed Rhett a washcloth. He held it open in his hands

and Cole quickly rubbed the hotel bar of soap across the terry cloth until it lathered. He took the soapy cloth from Rhett's hands and washed him thoroughly, making his way across Rhett's chest to his back and down between his legs.

His balls were heavy and Cole massaged them in his palm until Rhett moaned. The sound was gorgeous, a melody that Cole wanted to get used to hearing. Maybe Rhett was right. Real dating wasn't such a preposterous idea.

Rhett took the washcloth from his hand and dropped it on the floor between them. He reached for the soap and lathered his hands, slicking his palms up Cole's chest to his shoulders.

"I never want to stop touching you," Rhett admitted with a blush that quickly spread to his throat.

"Then don't," Cole conceded, echoing his reply from earlier in the night.

Maybe it was the romance of Tahiti, the scents in the air and the way the stars and moonlight reflected off the water that was all around them, but everything with Rhett seemed magical. Like something that had been born and nurtured in the depths of Cole's mind, then removed and constructed into complete perfection.

"You'd never get any work done," Rhett murmured, his hands dragging down Cole's ribs.

"That's fine," Cole assured him.

"You're ridiculous," Rhett teased, pushing Cole under the spray.

They both rinsed the soap from their bodies and dried off, returning to the bed together, still naked.

"What do you want to do now?" he asked, unsure of how to proceed.

"Like, immediately?"

"Obviously."

"Grab the champagne from the fridge, let's go sit outside." Cole pointed toward the small fridge in the corner of the room. Rhett snatched his underwear from the bed and put them on, shuffling to the fridge and grabbing the bottle.

Cole grabbed a pair of underwear out of his suitcase and stepped into them, following Rhett out of the room and onto the patio. He loved that their room was on the beach, the sand practically coming straight to their door.

Instead of sitting in one of the wooden chairs, Cole lowered himself to the step and sat, digging his feet into the still-warm sand. Rhett joined him, scratching the foil from around the neck of the bottle and twisting the cage away from the cork.

"Do the honors?" he asked, holding the bottle between them.

"Happily," Cole agreed, taking the bottle.

He angled it toward the ocean and worked his thumb under the cork, popping it free with a bang that echoed through the night. The bubbles overflowed and he laughed, raising the bottle to his lips and slurping the champagne before it was lost.

"Don't move," Rhett blurted, jumping up and running back into the room.

Cole didn't move, the bottle still in his mouth and the bubbles sliding down his hands. He waited, glancing toward the room and waiting for Rhett to reappear. When he did, he had a camera with him and he hopped off the deck and into the sand. He looked above him at the moon, then back at Cole.

He lifted the camera and squinted, looking through the viewfinder. Cole heard the camera click in rapid succession before Rhett lowered it and stared fondly at him.

"What?" he asked, daring to change his pose now that Rhett had his pictures.

"Just the way you looked," Rhett said, coming back to the patio and sitting beside Cole. He set his camera out of the way of the sand and bumped their shoulders together. "I didn't want to ever forget it."

Cole passed him the champagne and slid a hand around Rhett's waist. They sat there quietly, watching the moon dance on the water, passing the bottle between them until it was empty.

"Do we really have to go home?" Rhett whispered, burying the base of the bottle in the sand between their feet.

"Do you like it here that much that you'd want to stay?"

Cole closed his eyes, the stars spinning behind his eyelids like a merry-go-round.

"I like it with you."

"I'll be with you at home," Cole reminded him.

"But not like this." Rhett gestured behind him to the room they were sharing.

Cole kicked at the neck of the champagne bottle and stood up, tugging Rhett with him. He wrapped his arms around him and kissed him, gently and sweetly, his tongue sliding slowly against Rhett's mouth until he was allowed inside.

Rhett moaned into his mouth and Cole held him tighter, only separating so they could make it back into the room without falling over each other. The champagne had made Cole's limbs loose and his blood hot.

"Well, our relationship is very serious," Cole reminded him. "I wouldn't be surprised if a proposal was in your future."

Rhett smacked his chest and rolled his eyes. "What's your point?"

Cole figured it was all or nothing.

"It makes sense that if things are this serious, that when we get back to the valley," he said, pausing to swallow the last bit of fear, "my home becomes your home."

"Are you asking me to move in with you, Cole Mallory?" Rhett kissed Cole along his jaw, up to his ear.

"I am," Cole confirmed.

Rhett made a speculative sound, then his lip angled up into a smile. "My answer is yes."

Cole kissed him, faster and more urgent than on the sand. Rhett tangled his fingers into Cole's hair and they tumbled together into the bed.

Chapter Twenty

RHETT

Rhett woke the next morning pressed against Cole. The night before, they'd had sex again, then traded secrets in the dark until they were both too loopy from a toxic combination of champagne and exhaustion. The night had felt like a fairy tale to Rhett. As if he'd been the pauper, swept off his feet by the handsome prince. Tahiti was paradise, but Rhett was starting to feel like anywhere with Cole could be that for him.

Being allowed to wake up next to Cole the way he'd wanted to, for the first time, Rhett was eager to savor the moment. He snuggled closer, breathing deep and sighing happily when Cole's lips found his forehead.

"As cute as you were when you flung yourself halfway across the room, I have to admit I prefer this." Cole wrapped his arms around Rhett, tugging him closer.

His erection, which had more to do with Cole now than the fact that it was morning, pressed against Cole's leg and he found himself smiling against Cole's skin, the heat of lingering mortification sweeping over him. "I still can't believe I humped your leg."

"You humped a lot more than my leg last night."

"Mmhm," Rhett purred, stretching, sliding his hand across

Cole's abdomen. "I did. You did too." The night played again and again in his mind. A memory on an infinite loop that turned soft at the edges like a dream sequence.

"Rhett," Cole rasped his name in that scratchy sort of voice that Rhett had come to recognize as lust and what he hoped was affection. Cole rolled them over, kissing him far too tenderly, his body on top of Rhett's but not pressed hard against him the way he suddenly needed it to be.

Rhett grabbed Cole's face, deepening the kiss as he wrapped a leg around Cole and urged him closer. So much that had started out so fake had become so real. Rhett never expected to feel the way he did, as if he'd been walking next to a dream all his life and never realized it until he'd been forced to turn his head.

Cole moaned into his mouth, his body hard and hot against Rhett's. He kissed away the entire fabric of Rhett's existence. Everything was different now. For better or for worse, this was real and when the wheels hit the tarmac back in California, nothing would be the same.

Rhett had never been one to take risks, but Cole made it worth it. Cole's easy laughter, his ambition, his sense of humor, there wasn't a thing about Cole that Rhett didn't like.

Cole pulled out of the kiss, hot breath bursts against his shoulder as Cole buried his face there, kissing Rhett's neck. His shoulder. His clavicle. Cole sat up suddenly, aligning their cocks and wrapping a fist around them. "I have to be inside you." Desperation clung to Cole's words as he reached for the side table then dropped a condom on the bed.

Rhett grabbed the condom and Cole eyed him quizzically as he sat up, tearing the package open. "What are you doing?"

Rhett didn't say anything. He gazed at Cole, who was still just as beautiful as he'd been the night before, even with bedhead and eyes that were half sleepy, half lust-addled. He licked his lips and glanced down, then taking Cole's cock in his hand, he unrolled the condom onto it. Even Cole's cock was perfect, Rhett mused as Cole slanted his mouth over his and pushed him back down into the mattress. Rhett figured it to be slightly above average, but not so huge that he couldn't take it several times a day.

"Please," Rhett pleaded Cole, kissing the corner of his mouth.

"Now?" Cole's cock pressed against Rhett's hole.

"Now," he panted, sweat beading on his forehead. "I want to feel you the whole way home. I want to sit on the plane next to you and be able to tell you were there."

I want to know that this was real, even after Tahiti is a memory.

Cole, whether he understood Rhett's urgency for what it was or not, listened to his pleas and buried himself inside him.

Rhett came undone. His body didn't feel like it belonged to him in those moments. It was Cole's. The way he fucked him, hard, ferocious, not stopping their kiss, not coming up for air, not saying anything. The only sounds in the room were the slap of flesh, moans and whimpers, desperate breaths, and the roar of the ocean in the distance.

Unable to hold back anymore, Rhett wrapped his hand around his cock. Cole had kept him riding the edge of his orgasm, hard and fast, but never quite letting him go over. He whimpered at the first slide of his cock in his fist and his balls tightened. Cole swore, and Rhett stroked his cock again, the desperation in Cole's voice, the slight squeak in his words had Rhett coming, his orgasm slamming into him, shattering him as Cole continued to thrust into him, driving them both farther up the bed.

Cole's movements slowed and they still kissed. Slow slides of tongue and gentle nips of teeth against swollen lips, the kiss lasted until the cum on Rhett's stomach started to dry and Cole's cock slid out of his now tender ass.

Cole lay plastered against Rhett, still sprawled on top of him. Rhett drew his hands up and down Cole's back, raking his nails against his skin, enjoying the simple act of touching him.

"We should shower," Rhett said, but didn't move. Neither did Cole, who made a disapproving noise.

"If we keep showering every time we do that, Tahiti will run out of water."

Rhett laughed and hugged Cole to him. "I need at least fifteen minutes and some coffee and maybe something to eat. I'm starving."

"Fine, but room service."

Rhett didn't argue; he didn't particularly want to leave the room either. He was greedy for Cole's undivided attention.

"I'll order us some food while you clean up?" Cole asked, pushing himself off Rhett, but stealing a kiss before climbing out of bed.

"It's after noon already. Do you think they still serve eggs and bacon?"

"It's bacon and eggs," Cole corrected with a grin, as he headed for the bathroom to dispose of the condom. "But it's Tahiti, not a drive thru, I'm fairly certain that you can get breakfast whenever you want."

Rhett showered quickly, wrapping himself up in one of the fluffy hotel robes. He exited the bathroom and found Cole on the bed in matching terry-cloth.

By the time breakfast arrived, Cole had also freshened up and they ate in the room, enjoying the saltwater breeze and the ridiculous smiles on the other's face. Cole stood after breakfast and went back to the bed, stripping out of his robe. He tossed it aside and stretched out on top of the very rumpled bedcovers, demanding, "Show me your pictures."

Rhett shoved his empty plate aside and went to his suitcase, retrieving his camera and handing it to Cole. Then he let his robe slide to the floor in a heap before climbing in bed. He let Cole hold the camera and flip through the pictures at his leisure.

"I have other pictures on my phone, but these are mostly ones I took when you weren't with me."

"So this is what you did yesterday morning?" Cole mused thoughtfully as he scrolled through the images, stopping at the one that Rhett had taken of his feet in the sand.

"I never thought I'd say this," Cole looked at him, grinning. "You have really cute toes."

"Oh, my God, stop. I was bored, okay."

"So you took a picture of your feet?" Cole raised an eyebrow and Rhett felt his face get hot.

"I wanted to remember how the sand felt."

Cole's grin softened into a sweet sort of smile and he turned back to the camera, flipping to the next picture. "Tell me why you took this one?" Cole asked and Rhett explained. They continued that way, talking in hushed tones as Rhett showed Cole Tahiti the way he saw it.

Until they reached the picture of the flower pot he'd spied in the market, but hadn't bought.

Cole laughed. "Lucy would look adorable in that."

Rhett laughed and, for fun, turned his head and bit Cole's pectoral muscle. Cole fumbled the camera, and they both burst out laughing. Rhett took the camera and set it aside. He wasn't interested in pictures anymore. The only thing he was interested in was Cole.

"Are we really going to do that again? Already?" Cole asked as Rhett slid over top of him, straddling him.

"I can stop if you want," Rhett started to move, but couldn't, not with the iron grip Cole had on him then.

"That's the last thing I want."

⁂

Rhett lost track after that of how many times they'd kissed, how many minutes and hours they'd spent stowed away in that room, a perfect bubble in paradise where the rest of the world didn't exist.

Checking out the next morning was bittersweet. Tahiti had turned out to be more than he'd ever dreamed it to be, and he was returning home with more than he left with. A fake relationship that wasn't entirely fake anymore and feelings that were more real than anything he'd ever felt before.

The bright side of the return trip was that Kristen wouldn't be travelling with them. She and her new husband had booked an extended, and expensive, honeymoon that would take them around the world. She wouldn't be returning for three months, to both Rhett and Cole's delight.

At the airport, Rhett let Cole be the gentleman and handle their luggage. In turn, he bought them something to eat in the lounge after they'd passed through security. Rhett fished his phone out of his pocket and turned it on.

"Penny thinks I've died and that you fed my body to the sharks."

"Tell her it wasn't sharks. You were taken hostage by an errant street crab. I tried to save you, but it was a lost cause."

"I told her that you lost me at sea. I'm in a rubber dinghy with two percent power and she'll have to find a new babysitter for Tyson." Rhett tapped out an entirely different message, one that was fifty percent emoji and that gave away very little information.

"Already harassing you about me, is she?"

"You don't want to know," Rhett answered truthfully and he tried not to think about how different things were going to be when they landed back home. After they'd eaten, they sat next to each other, their hands linked, Rhett resting his head on Cole's shoulder. He drifted off, only waking when Cole shook him gently and told him their flight was boarding.

Rhett headed for the gate, boarding pass in one hand, Cole's in the other.

He already missed Tahiti.

Chapter Twenty-One
COLE

Rhett shuffled himself around in the doorway of Cole's house awkwardly.

"Are you coming in?" Cole asked, continuing through the house and into the kitchen. He grabbed a bottle of water from the fridge and waited for Rhett to close the door and come inside.

"How does this work?" Rhett asked him, finally in the kitchen.

Cole set the water on the counter and walked over to him. He grabbed his hips and pulled him close, sliding a hand around and pressing his fingers into the seam of Rhett's ass.

"Did I do a good job? Can you still feel me inside you?" he whispered, ignoring Rhett's question. Rhett groaned and pushed back on his hand.

"I can," Rhett whispered into his neck.

"That's how it works. You come live with me and you'll never have to worry about what it feels like to not be well used." He inhaled the delicious smell of Rhett's skin. "But I'm jet-lagged and I want to just rest, so come lie down with me."

Cole dropped his arm and grabbed Rhett's hand, leading him back through the house, up the stairs and into the bedroom. Cole undressed himself before removing every article of Rhett's clothing with the utmost care. He paid extra attention to his favorite parts of Rhett's body, laving gentle touches and soft glides of his lips across the bulging muscle in Rhett's shoulder, the sloping angle of his hip, before laying him down in bed.

Rhett kicked the blankets out of the way and made room for Cole, who lay down beside him. He pulled the blankets up to their chests and quickly fell asleep.

***

"What day is it?" Rhett mumbled, before sitting upright and shouting out an obscenity. Cole laughed and sucked, his tongue flat against the underside of Rhett's cock. He didn't know how long they'd slept, but the room was dark and Cole woke up with an unquenchable need to taste Rhett's dick in his mouth.

He hummed a greeting against Rhett's cock and hollowed his cheeks, bobbing his head up and down. Rhett's dick was magnificent. It was an easy handful with a graceful curve to the left just below the tip. The skin was pink and smooth, and so warm to the touch. He fingered Rhett's balls, teasing his hole with the tips of his fingers.

"You're gonna kill me," Rhett whispered, dropping back against the pillows with a huff. Cole shook his head and pushed a finger inside. He twisted his wrist and felt around until he grazed a soft bundle of nerves that drew another shocked cry from Rhett's throat.

Cole stroked Rhett's prostate while he sucked his cock, his face and Rhett's groin fully covered in spit.

"I'm gonna come," Rhett panted. "Gonna come."

Cole pressed against Rhett's prostate and hummed happily when Rhett cried out, tangling his fingers into Cole's hair. Rhett's cock pulsed and throbbed, hot jets of cum landing against the back of his tongue.

He eased his finger and his mouth away from Rhett at the same time, leaning back with a sleepy smile and a lick of his lips.

"Is this an every morning thing?" Rhett mumbled, arm thrown over his face.

Cole crawled up his body, laying half on top of him and half beside him. He stroked his fingers down Rhett's side, causing him to shiver. "It's not morning."

"I think you know what I meant." Rhett dropped his arm, wrapping it around Cole's shoulders. He smiled down at him and Cole's entire body felt warm.

"There will be frequent cocksucking, I assure you," Cole promised, uncertain of how this had become his life.

It was almost literally just yesterday when he'd been at Tubby's, lamenting the possibility of losing his livelihood to a stranger when Rhett and this harebrained idea fell into his lap. This fake relationship that probably hadn't ever been fake was terribly real now, the proof of it still slicking its way down the back of Cole's tongue.

He cleared his throat and pressed a kiss against Rhett's chest.

"I don't know what time it is, but I'm starving. Do you want to eat?" he asked, forcing himself away from Rhett's delicious body.

"I had a great time this week, but anything other than coconut, please," Rhett begged with a small laugh.

"No coconut, I swear." Cole stood and stretched, definitely catching Rhett checking out his ass. "Pizza or Chinese?"

"Oh, God. Pizza," Rhett said, rolling onto his side and watching Cole retreat into the bathroom.

Cole laughed and took a quick piss, washed his hands, then splashed some water on his face. He finger combed his hair back and returned to the bedroom, pulling his pajamas off the floor and putting them on.

"I don't even know where my phone is," he mumbled, looking around the room. "I think it's downstairs."

"Is it okay if I grab a shower?" Rhett asked, still lazing around the bed like a cat.

"Of course. It's your house now," Cole reminded him.

The easy smile on Rhett's face fell before he schooled his features back into something that resembled happiness.

"We're gonna talk about that face of yours as soon as I've gotten food ordered," Cole said, pointing at Rhett.

He knew this whole relationship between them hadn't moved as either of them had planned, but he'd be lying if he said he wasn't pleased with the turn of events. There had always been something that felt lacking when he'd dated other people. Whatever their gender, it had always been fun, but Cole had always felt like there was some sort of extra *oomph* that should have been there.

It never had been, but now it was.

As he walked downstairs, Cole thought of how different his life would have been if at any point in his youth he'd have just stopped and looked to Ryan's side and seen Rhett there— *really* seen him— for the boy he'd been or the man he was now.

Cole found his phone lying on the kitchen counter and he dialed the local pizza shop, ordering a large pepperoni for delivery. He tapped out a text to Ryan, letting him know that he was back safe from Tahiti then made his way into the living room. He turned the TV on, flicking through channels until he settled on an *I Love Lucy* rerun.

"This is my favorite show."

Rhett's voice from behind him made him jump. Cole raised a hand to his chest in fright and turned, finding Rhett lingering in the doorway.

"You scared the shit out of me," Cole admitted, the adrenaline in his body starting to settle once he realized there wasn't a threat present. "Come sit with me."

Cole patted the couch and turned, sliding back against the arm of the couch where he'd been sitting. Rhett didn't show up, so Cole twisted around and looked behind him.

"Is this a thing you've always done or is it just for me?" Cole asked, making a come here motion with his finger. Rhett walked into the room, taking the seat beside Cole.

"What do you mean?"

"You linger in doorways, like you're not sure if you should keep going or turn back," Cole told him, quickly shaking his head when he realized what a metaphor Rhett's continual hesitation was for their relationship.

Rhett eyed him speculatively and shrugged. "I wouldn't read too much into it if I were you."

"Yeah, that's not gonna work with me," Cole informed him, taking his hand and pressing soft kisses against his knuckles. "Between the weird faces you make at me and the doorway loitering, I can tell something isn't right with you and I want to know what it is. And if you want this fake relationship to be a real relationship, you're going to need to pony up."

Rhett pursed his lips together and stared at their joined hands. A minute, two, three. The silence growing between them.

"What are you scared of?" Cole whispered.

"Nothing," Rhett answered quickly, eyes snapping up to focus on Cole's worried face. "It's not like that."

"What is it like then?" Cole pressed, giving Rhett's hand a reassuring squeeze.

"This is crazy, right? We've known each other our whole lives and neither of us gave the other a second look, and now after a week of pretending to be with each other, we really are with each other?" Rhett paused. "I've loved the past three days, but none of that changes the fact you didn't even know I existed before then."

Cole chewed his lip between his teeth, hating the conflict that looked like it was tearing Rhett apart. Even when they'd planned on this being fake, he'd never wanted to make things worse for Rhett.

"I'm not going to change my mind," Cole assured him. He gripped Rhett's chin in his face and turned him so they were looking at each other. "Now that I've had you, I don't want to go back. I *won't* go back."

Cole pressed their mouths together, kissing Rhett with what he hoped was a convincing level of dedication to the newest development between them.

"You move between partners so fast," Rhett mumbled against his lips.

"None of them were you," Cole reminded him. "None of them ever made me feel the way you do."

Rhett nodded and dipped his head, cheeks coloring slightly.

"This is real, Rhett."

"Okay," Rhett conceded.

"Isn't it real for you?"

Rhett scoffed. "I think that's obvious."

"What does that even mean?" Cole asked with a small chuckle.

"Jesus, Cole. Look at you." Rhett swiped his hand through the air in front of Cole's chest.

"Look at me?" Cole barked out a laugh. "Look at you."

He pushed Rhett backward onto the couch and sucked one of his nipples into his mouth.

"Look at this sexy little pink nipple," he murmured against Rhett's tender flesh. He kissed his way down Rhett's ribs to the slight *V* where his muscles angled down to his cock. He licked a hot stripe across the skin. "Look at this muscle here, like an arrow showing me where to find what I've been looking for my whole life."

Cole took the waistband of Rhett's pants in his hands and lowered them slightly, exposing the curled hairs around the base of his cock. He pulled another inch. "Look at this cock. It's perfect and it hurts me so good that I can't stop coming."

Rhett's cock flexed against Cole's chin. He kissed his way back up Rhett's body, sliding his tongue through the grooves made by the muscles and bones until he reached Rhett's neck. He latched his mouth around the thin skin at the base of Rhett's throat and sucked a bruise onto his skin that would be visible to everyone.

Cole was not above marking his territory. He pulled away from his throat with a wet pop and licked his way up Rhett's chin to his mouth, dropping quick kisses across the surface of his lips. "And this mouth. Jesus, Rhett. This mouth makes me so hard."

Rhett's mouth parted and Cole swiped his tongue against his teeth before pulling away with a mischievous look. "I can't keep my hands off of you."

Rhett panted beneath him and smiled up, his eyes glassy with want. "You shouldn't then."

"But we need food," Cole complained weakly, forcing himself away. He sat on his hands and smiled over at Rhett innocently.

"You're no fun. You're a boring former fake boyfriend. Has anyone ever told you that?" Rhett pushed himself into a sitting position, getting comfortable in front of the TV again.

"Nope," Cole laughed. "That's one thing I've never been accused of."

The doorbell rang and Rhett jumped up. "I'll get it. I'm starving."

"My wallet is in the bowl by the door, just give him the blue debit card in front," Cole said, pointing toward the door.

Rhett saluted him and Cole smiled at his back, seeing those telltale patterned flush spots decorating Rhett's spine again. It made him irrationally happy that Rhett wanted him as badly as he did.

"Shit, I don't have a shirt on," Rhett said, turning around embarrassed with a hand over his chest.

"It's just the pizza guy," Cole reminded him with a roll of his eyes. He turned back to the TV.

Rhett pulled the door open and coughed, an awkward and terrified noise that had Cole looking toward the door again.

"Ryan, hey," Rhett choked out. "What's up?"

Chapter Twenty-Two

RHETT

Ryan's expression morphed from relaxed to tight and confused. It darkened a little as he raked his gaze over Rhett's naked torso.

Ryan cleared his throat as Cole came up behind Rhett. His arms slid around Rhett and he tugged him inside, away from the door. "Let your brother in. I ordered enough pizza for everyone."

"Heard you were back from Kristen's wedding." Ryan flashed a look at Rhett. "I still can't believe Macy gave you time off at the drop of a hat."

"It was..." Rhett cleared his throat. "It was good timing. Her niece got dumped on her for a few weeks and she's been helping out. Macy simply had her do more when I was away. It also helps that I've never asked for time off before."

Rhett tried to wriggle free of Cole's arms until he kissed him on the shoulder. "Stop," Cole whispered to him.

He let himself settle there in the safety of Cole's touch, although still not safe from the weight of Ryan's scrutiny. Rhett wasn't used to feeling as though he had anything to explain to anyone, certainly not to his brother, who mostly seemed not to care what Rhett did with his life. But Ryan and Cole had been friends since they were kids. Rhett didn't want to be the thing that came between them.

The doorbell rang again and this time Cole did let Rhett wriggle out of his arms. "I'll get the pizza," Rhett declared, still clinging to Cole's wallet. "You two go sit. I'll be right there."

Rhett took the interlude with the pizza guy, who very graciously did not stare at his naked chest, to calm his frazzled nerves. Cole had been doing a remarkable job of convincing him that he could belong here, that he wouldn't look away from Rhett now that he'd seen him. That he wasn't a mere passing interest, that he meant something to him.

It had been entirely too easy to believe him in the bubble that had become their lives. Ryan's sudden appearance shattered that bubble and instantly the real world was very much real again.

Rhett took a steadying breath and carried the pizza into the living room. He set it on the coffee table and was going to take a seat on the other end of the couch, but Cole leaned forward, grabbed Rhett's waist and hauled him down next to him.

"Let's eat, I'm starving." Cole kissed his cheek, then flipped the lid of the pizza box open. He pulled out two slices, holding one out for Rhett, who took it without hesitation.

Rhett became aware of Ryan's gaze gravitating between him and Cole and back again. Apparently, Cole also noticed. He swallowed a bite of pizza and looked at Ryan. "Stop gawking."

"This is weird," Ryan stated, waving his hand in the air, at them, at the pizza, at the television still turned to *I Love Lucy*.

"What's weird, Ryan?" Cole asked, and even Rhett had to grin at the sound of frustration Ryan made in the back of his throat.

"Really? My little brother is practically sitting in your lap, looking like you just...never mind, and you're watching *I Love Lucy* of all things."

Cole leaned back, tugging Rhett with him, snugging him next to his side. His fingers traced along his shoulder in small circles, but Rhett could feel the tension radiate off Cole.

"Ryan." His voice was even and smooth, but Rhett had the

distinct impression that Cole's tension was carefully restrained anger. He'd never seen Cole anything but relaxed and laid back. This new side of him made Rhett appreciate Cole's easily won smiles and laughter. "Do you love your brother?"

"What kind of a question is that? He's my brother."

Rhett leaned closer to Cole, watching Ryan's face carefully.

"And I'm your best friend, yes?"

Ryan's slice of pizza finished, he leaned back and crossed his arms defiantly over his chest. "Duh."

"Then shut up," Cole said, clearly exasperated. "Whatever chip you have on your shoulder about this, you need to get over it. Rhett and I are happy and he's moving in here, so you'll have to get used to us sooner or later."

"Moving in?" Ryan gaped for a minute, then looked at Cole. "So it's going to be the three of us hanging out now?"

"I do have a life you know, Ryan. I won't monopolize all of your best friend's time."

Cole leaned over, gripped his chin and turned Rhett to face him before stealing a chaste kiss.

"Maybe I want you to," Cole declared, sending a bloom of heat through Rhett.

His words now, said in front of Ryan, did more to soothe Rhett's fears that he was just a passing interest than his eager kisses had. Ryan was part of the real world, and if Cole still wanted Rhett now that the real world had crashed back into their lives, then he maybe really did want him.

"But you've never even had a boyfriend before," Ryan piped up and Rhett snapped his gaze over to him.

"He has one now, that's all that matters." Rhett suddenly wanted Ryan gone so he could kiss Cole. He'd start at his mouth and kiss every inch of him after that—down his spine to the center of his perfectly meaty ass and back again.

Ryan exhaled and looked slightly defeated, so Rhett tossed him a bone. "You know I won't hog your best friend all the time, right?

I still have to spend lots of time with Penny and Tyson, and most of the time I have a job to do."

"Whatever," Ryan sighed, reaching for another slice of pizza. "Don't hurt each other or I'll have to kick both your asses, okay?"

Cole laughed and kicked Ryan in the shin. "Like to see you try. I can still take you."

The conversation shifted into light teasing after that, who could take who, who would win and how. After three slices of pizza and another rerun of *Lucy*, Rhett yawned and moaned sleepily as Cole tugged him closer, his breath tickling Rhett's ear.

"Sleepy?"

"Mmhm. I work tomorrow too. I should go home and unpack."

"You should stay here and sleep in my bed with me. Besides, I picked you up, your car is at home. I'll take you to it tomorrow before work."

"So I'm your prisoner?"

Cole chuckled and Ryan coughed.

"That's my cue to leave, I guess." Ryan fished in his pocket for his keys and Rhett made no move to stand up, though Cole did to give Ryan a hug.

"Thanks for stopping by."

"Yeah," Ryan exhaled.

"We'll go for drinks or hang out soon." Cole slapped Ryan on the back and walked him to the door, returning to Rhett with a soft smile. "Let's get you upstairs and tuck you in."

Rhett heaved himself off the couch. "Tuck me in?"

Cole caught Rhett's wrist and pulled him close, their bodies slamming together, Cole grinning at him. "I wish our bedroom wasn't all the way upstairs. I can't get enough of you."

Then they were kissing. Cole's hands buried in Rhett's hair, his skin hot against Rhett, their hard cocks pressed against each other as Cole kissed Rhett with a dedication that Rhett had never experienced.

He pulled away, breathless, letting Cole tug him toward the

stairs. "You called it our room." Rhett felt dizzy from the kiss and the way his life had spun itself not out of control, but into something he hardly recognized but wanted. He wanted this, this impossible life that two weeks ago didn't exist, that one week ago was a fake, and had since become the most real thing in Rhett's life.

They landed in a tangled heap of limbs on the bed—their bed —Rhett corrected himself.

"If we're really doing this, Cole," Rhett breathed as Cole made more marks on Rhett's skin.

"Not if. We are," Cole replied, nipping at Rhett's skin.

He squawked indignantly and wriggled, but was held still by Cole's firm grasp. "We need to get tested."

Cole stilled. Exhaled. "Oh fuck, yes. Tomorrow. I'll go tomorrow." Cole lifted his head and looked at Rhett, promising once again, "Tomorrow."

※

Tomorrow came the way days always did, but slightly different because, as Cole had promised before, Rhett felt perfectly used. He didn't mind topping when the mood struck him, as it had their first time together in Tahiti, and he wanted to do it again, but not right now. Right now he wanted to lie in Cole's arms their first morning together, truly together.

"If I remember correctly," Cole's husky voice sent shivers down Rhett's spine. He didn't say another word. Instead he flipped Rhett onto his back and sank down under the covers, peppering Rhett's body with kisses. He moaned, yanking the blankets out of the way so he could see as Cole gazed up at him. He watched his cock disappear into Cole's mouth, down to the root, and Cole still stared up at him.

Rhett sank his fingers into Cole's hair, not to control or force the speed, but to anchor himself. Cole closed his eyes, his dark lashes fanning out against his cheeks as they hollowed out. The sight of his cock in Cole's mouth should have been too lewd to be as beautiful as Rhett found it.

Cole sucked him with expert precision, passion, and moans that Rhett felt vibrate through his entire body and before long, Rhett was shouting, his hips thrusting, fucking himself with Cole's mouth, emptying his release down Cole's throat.

Cole climbed up Rhett's body afterward and grinned down at him, a wicked twinkle in his eye. "Good morning."

"You have ruined me." Rhett pressed his lips to Cole's, swept his tongue into his mouth and caught the taste of his own release.

"I have to get home," he said, burying his face against Cole's shoulder. "I need to change, and call Penny and get ready for work, but I have time to return the favor in the shower."

"It's not a favor that you need to return, Rhett." Cole pinched the bit of skin above Rhett's hip as he kissed him.

"I know, but maybe I want to taste you, too," Rhett admitted, brushing his lips against Cole's.

They showered together, somehow getting clean without spending too much time kissing and stealing touches, or trading gropes. Rhett did return the favor, sinking to his knees in the tiled shower, licking the water from Cole's skin before taking his cock into his mouth. Cole braced his hands on either side of the shower and stared down at Rhett the whole time, commanding him to not look away from him.

Cole came first, spilling down Rhett's throat, then hauling him up, plunging his tongue greedily into Rhett's mouth. He shoved him up against the wall of the shower and wrapped a hand around Rhett's cock, dragging another orgasm out of him.

It was a miracle they made it out of Cole's house and down to Rhett's apartment at all. Cole walked Rhett to the door, carrying his luggage for him. Rhett unlocked his door and Cole followed him inside.

"Lucy," Cole called, "Daddy's home."

Rhett punched Cole in the arm playfully, and Cole fought back by hauling Rhett in for another kiss. He put his hands against Cole's chest. "Cole. Work. Job. Life. Friends. Remember those?"

Cole moaned, "Don't want to."

"Sorry, babe, we have to."

Cole sighed and kissed him one more time before reluctantly pulling away. "Okay, you win." He reached the door before pausing, keys in one hand, doorknob in the other. "Have dinner with me tonight?"

"Yes. But I don't think I can come for at least the next twenty-four hours."

Cole crossed the room and kissed Rhett again with a smirk. "See you later."

Rhett exhaled when the door clicked shut behind Cole and he tried his best not to feel morose or bereft at the sudden departure of his boyfriend. He looked at Lucy, who sat there lacking judgement, and exhaled sharply.

"Lucy, life is very weird. You should be happy you're a plant."

Chapter Twenty-Three
COLE

Three days later, Cole was at his desk when an email pinged alerting him to an incoming message. The subject line revealed it was a new posting on his medical chart. He quickly downloaded the file, pleased but not surprised to see the results all indicating negative. He forwarded the email to Rhett with some suggestive emojis before leaning back in his chair and stretching his legs.

"You all set for our two o'clock?" Elena, the product development manager for the vineyard asked, strolling into his office with her arms full of folders and paper.

"Of course," he answered, clearing space on his desk for her to set down everything she'd brought with her.

"I've got to tell you, Cole, sparkling wine isn't easy." Elena flopped into the chair and pushed a brown curl out of her eye.

"Bubbly wine," he corrected.

She waved a hand between them dismissively. "You have a few options."

"Alright, let's hear it."

"There's basically three ways you can make a wine sparkling, and it depends on what kind of bubbles you want to get and what kind of grapes you want to use."

"Do we need to plant new vines?"

"No. You can use the pinot noir grapes for the rosé you asked about, but aside from that, there's three ways you can ferment." She passed some documents over to him.

He glanced at them briefly before asking, "Do we need to get Laurence involved?"

Cole glanced at the calendar, trying to see if the production manager had any time he'd be able to sit down and hammer through the best course of action on this.

"Well, yes. But we can discuss this at a high level then go back to him once you know what you want to do."

"Awesome. Go on then, three ways?"

"Yeah," Elena said, reaching across his desk and tapping a fingernail on one of the pamphlets she'd given him. "So, Charmat, which ferments the fastest; champagne, which actually ferments in the bottle; and the bulk method, which basically just shoots air into the wine."

"That sounds..." Cole searched for the word. "Not appealing."

"Right," she agreed.

"Okay, then. Charmat and traditional."

"Charmat is sweet, like Asti."

"Mmmn," Cole approved.

"You do love the sweet wine."

"I do."

"And then the traditional method, which uses the final bottle as its own little fermentation tank. But this needs an additional fifteen to sixty months to ferment properly."

Cole whistled in disbelief. "I'm not one to cut corners, but Charmat is a viable and acceptable method?"

"Definitely," she confirmed, "I mean, Asti."

Cole laughed. "Point taken."

"Sooooo..." Elena grabbed some of the pamphlets out of his hand and shuffled around the papers between them, shoving a handful toward him and pulling the rest back into her arms. "This is what you're going to want to look at, then we can loop Laurence in and make plans for installation and production. The capital expenditure for the new equipment shouldn't be too bad compared to the operating budget. Oh! And we need to get Scott involved too, for marketing."

"Sounds good, Elena. I'll read it all over. I appreciate the time you put into everything."

"No thanks necessary, Cole, it's my job." Elena smiled at him, relaxing slightly. "So, how was Kristen's wedding?"

Cole loudly exhaled, flapping his lips together. "It was a lovely photo op."

Elena barked out a laugh, then quickly covered her mouth with her hand. "I hear you brought a date."

He raised an eyebrow. "Did you now?"

"Word travels fast, especially when the most eligible Mallory bachelor is involved."

"I'm the only Mallory bachelor," he reminded her dryly.

"Exactly. So, Rhett Kingston?"

"Rhett Kingston." Cole's breathing hitched as he said Rhett's name and he chuckled, well aware of just how much this man had taken over his life in such a short time. He remembered how reluctantly he'd crawled out of bed this morning, leaving a sleepy Rhett under the covers. Cole had drank his coffee in the kitchen and watered Lucy, who now sat proudly on the windowsill over the sink.

Rhett wasn't moved in yet, by any stretch of the imagination, but he'd brought over the important things. His camera, his e-reader, and his plant. Hopefully, when the weekend rolled around, they'd have an opportunity to move more of his things over, but that was assuming Rhett wasn't tied up with work.

"That's unexpected," Elena said, tilting her head in doubt.

"Why?"

"You've known him your whole life and there's never been anything between the two of you. What changed?"

Cole sucked the corner of his bottom lip into his mouth. "I

have another meeting in a few minutes, Elena. I'll have to cut this short."

"Right," she agreed, standing up and taking all of her papers and pamphlets with her.

Cole mentally chastised himself for being as standoffish as he had been about the sudden change in his relationship status with Rhett, realizing that he couldn't be so dodgy if he expected people to take him seriously. The relationship with Rhett was genuine now, so there wasn't really a need to lie. The only fallacy he had to keep track of was a fake anniversary date of June 12th.

"I did," he blurted out, truthfully, before Elena reached the door to his office.

She cast a glance over her shoulder. "What?"

"You asked what changed," he elaborated. "It was me."

She smiled at him, her eyes crinkling softly around the edges. "That's really sweet, Cole."

He shot her a fake scowl. "God, stop. Get out of my office now."

She laughed and closed the door behind her. Cole let out a rushed breath and tapped the screen on his phone to light it up. He didn't really have another meeting coming up; he was clear for the rest of the afternoon.

He had a reply message from Rhett, a scandalous looking picture of his midsection and thighs with a strategically placed fold of Cole's sheets across his groin. Cole shoved the heel of his hand against the base of his dick, trying to convince himself now was not the right time to get a boner.

Thankfully, his office phone rang.

"Mallory Vineyard, this is Cole," he answered.

"Cole," greeted his grandfather, Jacob, "how are you doing today?"

"I'm doing well, Pops, thank you. How are you? You and Nan recovering from the jet lag all right?" Cole picked up a pen and doodled circles across the bottom of his desk calendar.

"Oh, you know how your Nan is," he said noncommittally.

Cole chuckled in lieu of verbalizing an answer.

"How are things at the vineyard?" his grandfather asked.

"Really well," Cole enthused. "I actually just met with Elena about a new product I want to develop so we're going to rope Laurence in next week and get the ball rolling."

"Huh. Is now a good time for that?"

There was a hesitation in his grandfather's voice that made him shift uncomfortably in his seat. He'd always been supportive of the decisions Cole made around the vineyard.

"Why wouldn't it be?" Cole questioned. "It was actually Rhett's idea. Mallory Bubbly Wines."

"Ah, yes. Rhett. It seems like you've been giving him a lot of leeway over there, Cole."

Cole grimaced. "We were talking one night and he asked why Mallory didn't have any sparkling options and the idea really just took off from there. Elena thinks it's doable with little capital and Rhett and I really think the market is there."

"He has no experience with wine," Cole's grandfather protested.

"I do."

"Just make sure you take your time and think it through for yourself."

"I know, Pops. I've been at it here for seven years," Cole reminded him.

"What is the history with this Rhett boy?" his grandfather asked, changing the subject.

"We're dating," Cole summarized.

"Since when?"

"June," Cole bit out, before deciding to add, "twelfth."

"He's that Kingston boy's brother?"

"Well, first off, neither of them are *boys*," Cole emphasized. "And since he and Ryan are twins, they're both Kingstons, yes."

"Weird they're both gay," his grandfather remarked casually.

Cole inhaled an annoyed breath, not interested in going into details about genetics and sexual preferences with his seventy-eight year old grandfather.

"Pops, I have a meeting to get to. Is there anything you needed from me right away?" Cole asked, ready to end this awkward inquisition.

"Nope," his grandfather answered. "Just wanted to see how things were going with the grapes."

Cole couldn't stop himself from laughing at the casual way his grandfather always referred to the vineyard as *the grapes*. Then he swallowed it down when he realized the majority of the call had focused around Rhett and not the grapes at all.

"Sounds good, Pops," he said quickly. "We'll talk soon then."

Cole hung up and grabbed his cell phone, scrolling back to the picture Rhett had sent him before sending a reply.

Me: Are you still in bed?
Rhett: No, I took that this morning.
Me: What other dirty pictures are you stockpiling over there?
Rhett: Oh, you wouldn't believe the hoard I've accumulated.
Me: Are you going to be around when I'm off work?
Rhett: When are you off work? ;) ;) ;)
Me: An hour.
Rhett: I suppose I can make myself available.
Me: Can I cook for you?
Rhett: I don't know, can you?
Me: I have this new vegan steak recipe I want to try out on someone.

Rhett sent him a picture of his middle finger. Cole laughed, his lip quirking up into a sincere smile. He'd never felt the way Rhett made him feel and it just solidified that he'd done the right thing by not getting serious with anyone else in his past. No one had the spark Rhett did, no one made his insides feel like mush, no one made his cock as hard as steel.

Rhett: You make me want to actually go vegan just to spite you.
Me: I have some meat you can eat. *eggplant emoji*
Rhett: Oh! Speaking of...

Cole waited while a picture loaded on his screen. He was hoping for another lewd photo of his boyfriend, maybe with some fingers shoved up his ass, but what he got was twice as good—a printout from the clinic with Rhett's negative test results.

Me: I'm going to fill you up with my cum tonight.
Rhett: You better.

Cole turned his computer off and locked his desk. He grabbed his jacket from the back of his door and practically jogged to his car. He was ready to go home and show Rhett just what it meant to be well used.

Chapter Twenty-Four
RHETT

"You didn't have to sacrifice your child-free time to help me pack." Rhett said to Penny as she carefully stacked books into a box.

"Rhett, I have three hours and no kid. Doing anything while not smelling of spit-up is a miracle, even if it's helping you move into your boyfriend's house." Penny gave him a look from the corner of her eye. "Speaking of which, you and Cole Mallory? Since fucking when?"

"A few months ago. We kept it quiet." Rhett hated lying to Penny, but it was for the greater good.

"You didn't have to keep it a secret from me, Rhett."

He turned this comment over in his mind as he taped another box closed and wrote *books* on the outside in black marker. "It was important to us." It frightened Rhett sometimes how willing he'd been to lie to people for Cole, how expert he'd become in the art of half-truths. Other things, like his feelings for Cole, frightened him more than a few basically harmless lies.

"Aww, Rhett, I only want you to be happy. It's your relationship; you're allowed to keep it as private as you want. But I'm here if you need anything." Penny's smile sparkled. "Speaking of needing things, are you still up for watching Tyson so David can take me out for our anniversary?"

"Of course I am." Rhett's phone chimed with a text. He expected it to be Macy, finalizing his hours for the coming weekend. She was booked solid and, for the first time, Rhett actually minded being busy the entire weekend. He tried not to think about all the hours he wouldn't be with his boyfriend when he finally dug his phone out of his pocket.

Instead of Macy, the clinic texted him with his test results. Negative, as he'd expected. Rhett went from annoyed to horny and annoyed in two seconds flat and without thinking, he sent a text to Cole. He'd been lonely and bored all alone in Cole's bed that morning and had entertained himself with a variety of selfies he'd intended to save and send later.

"You're abandoning me, aren't you?" Penny asked, taping a box shut.

Rhett's face heated. "Maybe. Yeah, okay. I am. Not much more will fit in my car anyway." Rhett looked around at his apartment. He'd been coming here during the day while Cole worked and had packed most of his stuff. With Penny's help, he'd finished the rest of it. "I hate to run out on you, though."

Penny lifted a box, Rhett carried two, and she followed him out to his car. "Rhett, all I've ever wanted is for you to be happy, and you look happy. So if you're waiting for a protest or an inquisition, you'll be disappointed." Penny glanced at her watch. "I have another half an hour of freedom; I think I'll run and get a coffee."

Penny hugged him briefly, kissing his cheek before climbing into her car, waving a hand out her window as she drove away. Rhett filled his car with boxes and drove home, surprised, but only slightly, to see Cole's car already in the driveway.

Rhett carried a box into the house and set it down in the foyer. "How many laws did you break to beat me here?"

Cole appeared with a dazzling smile Rhett liked to pretend was reserved exclusively for him. He wrapped Rhett up in his arms and kissed him, long and deep. He moaned as Cole released him.

"You're going to make me burn dinner. Unpack your car and take a shower. You've got time."

"What are you making? Whatever it is, it already smells delicious."

"It's a surprise. Now go unpack your car before I pin you to the wall and take you right now."

Rhett stole a kiss.

"I wouldn't be opposed to that," he offered, turning for the door.

"You deserve better than a frantic fuck in a foyer, Rhett."

Rhett's heart constricted and he grinned, hopefully hiding how much the sentiment meant to him. "I bet you say that to all the boys."

"Only you, Rhett." Cole blew him a kiss, then disappeared back into the kitchen.

Rhett hated that Cole could make him blush so easily, but he'd started to become accustomed to the way his face would heat up and the way his insides would flutter. He secretly hated none of it. There wasn't a single thing about Cole that Rhett didn't find perfect or fascinating. He sometimes couldn't believe that he'd spent his whole life next to someone like Cole Mallory and hadn't ever thought of wanting more from him.

Rhett mused on this while he unpacked his car, stacking the boxes out of the way in a spare room with the others. He showered, taking his time to enjoy it. Cole's house never ran out of hot water it seemed, and Rhett could spend forever under the spray, but being naked and thinking of his boyfriend was often something that led to Rhett having an orgasm, so he finished his shower off without touching himself and dressed in a pair of fitted jeans and a shirt that he'd purchased for a date he'd never gone on. It was blue like the ocean in Tahiti and Rhett loved the feel of the fabric against his skin.

Rhett found Cole in the dining room. He'd set their places opposite to each other at the eight seater table. "You cooked a feast." Rhett grinned when Cole pulled his chair out for him.

"Did you know that this is the first time I've used this room?"

"Really?" Rhett asked, even though Cole's question was likely rhetorical.

Cole poured him a glass of red and nodded. "Never had a reason to use it before."

The table setting was simple, nothing extravagant, but it was the normalcy that sent a thrill through Rhett. How perfectly normal it felt to sit down in the dining room with Cole. To watch him pour a glass of wine for him and ask about his day while Rhett looked at the fare on his plate. Grilled steak and Caesar salad. Rhett knew what dessert was and though he wanted to eat slowly, savor every bite, and wring every bit of conversation out of Cole that he could, he also wouldn't complain too loudly if Cole decided to fuck him on the vacant side of the table.

"Are you all moved in?" Cole inquired, taking a sip of his wine, staring at Rhett over top his glass.

"Almost." Rhett frowned. "There's a couple more loads of boxes, and the furniture, but we don't really need the furniture."

"There's probably room for it in the garage if you wanted to keep it. Or we could get rid of some of mine, incorporate yours a bit. Whatever you want, Rhett."

Rhett shrugged a shoulder. "My stuff wouldn't look all that great in here. Besides, I'm not attached. It's just furniture. But it does seem a shame to let it rot in the garage. Do you know any young people just starting out who might need stuff?"

"I can ask around at work. Until then, we can store it in the garage. I can move it over when you're working this weekend. I'll make your brother help me."

Rhett sighed. "For the first time in my life, I hate working on the weekends." Before Cole, Rhett hadn't minded working all weekend. He hadn't minded having built-in excuses to not go away for weekends with his boyfriends. He didn't mind that his schedule often meant that he'd spend less time with his partners. He told himself that it made the time they did spend together even more precious.

But none of that was true with Cole. It made him sound pathetic and clingy, he thought, but he hated the idea that Cole had to work all week, and he had to work all weekend, leaving them with only bits of time together. Moments snatched from their busy lives wasn't enough to satisfy Rhett, who wanted to bask in the glow of this relationship.

"How is this going to work?" Rhett asked, slicing off another bite of his steak. "You work all week. Events almost always happen on the weekends. We'll never see each other."

Cole mulled the comment over for a minute. "Well," he started, and Rhett could almost see the gears turning in his head. "You could be the official Mallory Vineyard event coordinator. If people want to get married at Mallory, they'd have to use you. And you'd, of course, have staff, and there wouldn't be a wedding every weekend. It's an option, but think of it this way. You always have a venue, your father owns the linen rental company, so naturally you'd use him. Mallory hosts a couple of large events every year and we always hire an event coordinator for those anyway. If we had someone on staff, it would make that a lot less of a hassle for me. I could work with you. I think I'd like having you around all the time." Cole took another sip of his wine. "But if you'd rather start your own company, we'll make it work. This might be a good start, but whatever you want, Rhett."

"You just want me around so we can have all the office sex you want."

"So that's a yes?" Cole chuckled.

Rhett didn't even have to think about it. "Yeah, that's a yes."

"Excellent. And to launch the career of the official Mallory Vineyard event coordinator, you can plan our wedding."

Rhett had always wanted to be married at Mallory in the spring, but now he'd take any date at all. The date didn't matter half as much as the person he'd be marrying. "I can't wait." Rhett squeaked a little, then stared at his mostly empty plate. He lifted his gaze. "I think I've eaten enough."

Cole stood at the same time Rhett did. He grabbed the bottle of wine and Rhett's hand, and they walked upstairs together. Rhett practically trembled thinking of how it would feel when Cole slid inside of him bare for the first time. He'd finally know how it would feel to be marked by Cole Mallory. He felt oddly happy, as if Cole would be claiming him forever.

Cole tugged Rhett into his room, their room now, and set the wine on the dresser. His hand came up to Rhett's face, as it often did, and Rhett let himself lean into the touch. He thought Cole might say something, and though part of him was dying to know what Cole was thinking in that moment, he didn't ask.

Instead, he leaned in and kissed Cole, wrapping his arms around his neck, moaning into his mouth, pressing their erections together, using his body to beg for his touch on his skin, to beg for the feeling that overtook Rhett whenever Cole was near him like this. The way Cole fucked Rhett left him feeling happy and sated, well used, and treasured all at once. Cole always held him after, stroked his heated skin, kissed wherever he could reach—his forehead, his lips, his shoulders.

Cole looked at him as if he were important. He kissed him as if he were a treasure, and he fucked him as if they'd die if he stopped.

Rhett thought they just might.

He kissed Cole, parting his lips, allowing Cole's tongue inside his mouth and he wondered when he had let Cole inside his heart.

Chapter Twenty-Five
COLE

"Please tell me I can get inside of you," Cole mumbled into Rhett's mouth, walking him backward toward the bed.

Cole had spent the majority of the past week inside of Rhett, but the thrill of being able to take him bare for the first time had his skin electrified. Cole pulled his shirt over his head and quickly stepped out of his pants, gripping Rhett's shirt and tugging it over his head. The body Rhett had kept hidden from him all these years was a sight.

He wasn't overly toned, which made sense considering how much time he spent with his nose in a book, but the lines of his body were tight and firm, his skin stretched smooth over the dips and curves of his muscles. Cole popped the button on Rhett's pants, pushing them and his briefs to the floor, dragging his fingers along Rhett's soft thighs as he went.

Standing there with nothing between them, Cole swallowed, choking down the overwhelming desire to fuck Rhett through the floor until cum spilled out of him and he begged for Cole to stop. He steadied himself and kissed Rhett softly, teasing his lips with his tongue until Rhett's cock poked insistently against Cole's stomach.

"I have a confession to make," Cole whispered, laying Rhett down onto the bed softly. He reached for the bedside table, producing a bottle of lube. He slicked his fingers and teased Rhett's hole, easily pushing one, then two fingers inside. Rhett arched off the bed, sweat already beading against his temple as Cole worked him slowly, scissoring his fingers apart to stretch him.

"What?" Rhett panted, his voice soft and eager.

Cole removed his fingers and lubed his cock, pressing the head against Rhett's entrance and taking a steadying breath. He could feel Rhett give way, the ring of muscle at his entrance grabbing for the tip of his dick.

Cole wasn't convinced his heart wasn't going to slam out of his chest and explode between them. Rhett writhed underneath him, silently begging for penetration. He looked like a dream—slightly tan skin against Cole's crisp, white sheets, not to mention the feral noises tumbling from his mouth that grew louder every moment Cole wasn't inside of him.

"Look at me," Cole whispered, and Rhett's eyes flew open. Cole took a handful of deep breaths, petting his hands along Rhett's thighs, up to his ribs.

"I know that you doubt me," Cole continued. "You moved your things in, but I can tell that you don't think I'm all in."

Rhett squeezed his eyes closed and shook his head quickly against the pillow. "It's not that," he protested.

"It is though," Cole countered, using the head of his cock to stretch Rhett's hole without actually pushing inside. They both inhaled matching, sharp breaths. "And that's okay. I understand. I know I've been a certain way before, with other people."

Cole danced his fingers along the goosebumped skin of Rhett's thighs, his cock leaking precum against the rim of Rhett's ass. He could feel the slick slide from his dick and pool against him.

"I'll get there," Rhett said, and it sounded like he was imploring Cole to believe him, which was a ridiculous thing. Rhett was too good for Cole, and they both had to know that. Rhett who was so smart, and talented, and driven, and Rhett who looked like he should be cast in bronze when he came because his face was sheer perfection.

"*I'll* get there," Cole promised. "I'll deserve you, for real."

Rhett swallowed, the sound so loud it drowned out the beating of Cole's heart in his ears. He slid a hand up Rhett's chest and found their hearts were frantically in sync.

"What did you want to confess?" Rhett rasped, fisting his dick and squeezing around the base.

Cole gripped himself, looping his thumb and forefinger around his shaft and notching the tip of his cock against Rhett's ready hole.

"I've never done this before," he admitted, easing his way into Rhett's heat. Cole's body jerked forward, his hips slapping forward and instinctively burying himself as deep as he could reach.

"What?" Rhett's eyes widened and focused on him, even as his lashes fluttered from the penetration.

Cole lay his body over Rhett's, their hearts connected through their chests and he whispered his confession once again into Rhett's parted mouth. "I've never been with someone like this. Bare."

Rhett groaned and his muscles tightened around Cole's cock at the same time his arms wrapped around his back. Rhett pulled him closer, impossibly so, and slammed their mouths together. He kissed Cole with what Cole imagined to be...everything.

"Move," Rhett panted into his mouth after coming up for air, "I need to feel you move."

Cole parted their bodies reluctantly, fucking his way slowly in and out. Rhett arched up to meet him, his ass coming off the bed and his muscles clinging to Cole's cock when he retreated in a way that Cole hadn't ever felt in his life.

"You feel so good. So hot and tight," Cole praised, finding a rhythm that he could maintain without shooting his load in the first five minutes.

He fucked Rhett, even though it felt more like what Cole had always imagined making love would be. There on his bed, their bed, in the damp and tangled sheets, Cole took what Rhett offered him with no regret and no remorse.

Rhett's hand quickened around his cock and his face looked pained. His skin flushed and he cried out, jets of cum pooling against his chest. Cole leaned down and licked him clean, grabbing Rhett's thighs and laying into him the way he'd meant to earlier. He fucked Rhett so thoroughly the headboard creaked and the fitted sheet came loose. He fucked Rhett until he was begging for less, and more, and everything, his cock hard again between them.

"Come for me again," Cole requested, wrapping Rhett's hand around his cock. "Show me how good I make you feel."

His hips snapped forward and he circled them around, the tip of his cock sliding over Rhett's swollen prostate.

"It's too much," Rhett protested, even as he dutifully jerked himself.

"I know," Cole agreed, chin dropping to his chest. His balls were hot and tight, and ready to release themselves. "Now, baby. Do it now."

Rhett squeezed his eyes closed and matched Cole's pace, fucking his fist even as he writhed and groaned underneath Cole. Their bodies were covered in sweat and the residue of Rhett's earlier orgasm lingered on Cole's tongue.

"I'm gonna come inside of you," Cole whispered, still in awe of what was happening between them.

Rhett bore down, his muscles grabbing at Cole's cock and Cole watched cum dribble from between Rhett's grasp as he came for a second time. Cole shouted, throwing his head back in what felt like victory, his cock pumping spurts of his hot release as deep into Rhett as he'd ever been.

This was surreal—this primal mating between the two of them ignited a fire in Cole that he hadn't even known existed. His body bucked and trembled and he collapsed, riding through his orgasm as Rhett's arms and legs wrapped around him and held him tight.

He was aware of Rhett's voice in his ear, but couldn't make out the words. They sounded happy though; tired but pleased, and Cole closed his eyes, drifting off to an unexpected sleep.

※

"You need to wake up." Rhett's voice was soft and gentle in his ear. Cole groaned and rolled over, burying his face into his pillow.

"Why?" he groaned, unwilling to blink his eyes open.

"You're going to be late for work," Rhett told him.

"How? It's nighttime," Cole mumbled, sliding over and nuzzling his face in Rhett's armpit.

"It's not. It's six in the morning."

Cole's eyes flew open and he rolled away, searching for his phone on the nightstand. How was it morning? He didn't even remember going to bed. He and Rhett had eaten dinner and then come upstairs and had the best sex of Cole's life, and then....

"You fell asleep on me," Rhett informed him with a chuckle.

"I don't sleep," Cole said, confused. He sat up, the sheets gathered around his waist. He scratched his scalp with dull fingernails and looked at the clock which indicated Rhett was telling the truth. It was the next day.

"Well, you've obviously been having sex wrong until last night because you came and then passed the fuck out." Rhett laughed and leaned against the headboard as Cole scrambled out of bed in search of a clean towel and clothes to wear.

The words Rhett had said registered in his head and he stopped dead in his tracks. He pivoted back toward the bed and crawled up Rhett's body, gripping his chin between his thumb and forefinger. Rhett's face was playful, but turned serious the longer Cole held him there.

"Last night was right," Cole said solemnly. He swallowed his fear about the next words he was about to say, well aware he was talking to someone who very well still had one foot out the door. "It was right because it was you."

Before Rhett could reply, Cole backed off the bed and retreated to the shower, turning the hot on full blast and stepping under the spray. The water was instantly warm, which made Cole appreciative of the tankless water heater he'd paid to have installed last year. He washed himself quickly, shampooed his hair, and rinsed all the bubbles away.

When he stepped out of the shower, he found Rhett sitting on the bathroom counter, feet dangling and heels banging into the cabinet door under the sink.

"What are you going to do today?" Cole asked, wrapping the towel around his waist and situating himself between Rhett's legs. He looked in the mirror over Rhett's shoulder and finger combed his hair.

Rhett reached up and swatted Cole's hands away, arranging the strands and working through a few snarls with a much more delicate touch than he had. The perfect domesticity of the moment sat well with Cole, and he was completely aware of how *not* rattled the whole thing made him.

When Rhett finished paying his hair attention, Cole kissed him, easily and assuredly, hoping to tell him *I meant what I said last night. This is right. This is good. This is perfect.*

"Maybe I'll go through the pictures from Kristen's wedding or go through my boxes," Rhett answered when the kiss was over.

"You don't need to," Cole assured him. "You can just relax, or stay in bed, or whatever. Or you can come to work with me and I can run you up to human resources and get you hired."

Cole nipped at the skin of Rhett's throat, the hickey he'd left while they were in Tahiti fading now. Rhett groaned and the sound vibrated against Cole's mouth.

"Can I come by after lunch?" Rhett asked.

Cole nodded, inhaling the smell of their mingled sweat in the crook of Rhett's neck. "That's fine," he murmured, forcing himself away so he could see Rhett's face.

"Do we have plans tonight?" Rhett asked, again gently weaving his fingers through Cole's damp hair.

"No. Why?"

Rhett grinned deviantly, and Cole's cock twitched at the sight of it.

"Good," Rhett responded, tongue swiping across his lower lip. "I kind of can't wait to fuck my boss."

Chapter Twenty-Six
RHETT

"Ryan is sending over the samples of the new linens he ordered. The whole batch will be here before New Year's, but he's told me that we'll be impressed with the quality. As a bonus, they resist stains better and are easier to clean, cutting costs for them, and us, in return."

"By how much?" Cole asked, typing something into his laptop.

"Ryan is sending his projections over with the samples." Rhett listened as Elena inquired about a distribution hiccup that needed to be ironed out before the launch of the sparkling wine.

Rhett's employment at Mallory Vineyard was only a couple months old, and he felt as if he was still learning the ropes. He'd planned a couple of smaller events at the vineyard and had teamed up with Ryan, who was working with their father, to handle the linens.

"I think that about covers everything," Cole said, standing up. Everyone else did so and gathered their belongings off the conference table. "Mr. Kingston, can you stay behind, please? I need to discuss a few things with you."

Rhett nodded. Their relationship was hardly a secret and he

got a few knowing looks as people filed out of the room, but he didn't care.

When everyone left, Rhett looked expectantly at Cole. "You wanted to speak to me, Mr. Mallory?"

Cole's lip quirked. "Yes, actually. I wanted to go over the details for the New Year's launch of the sparkling wine. Walk me to my office."

Rhett pulled up the notes app on his tablet and read from his notes as they made their way to Cole's office down the hall. "I've received approximately three hundred RSVPs for the event."

"How many invites did you send?" Cole opened the door to his office and let Rhett enter first.

"Three hundred." Rhett grinned. "Ryan's giving us a great rate on all linen rentals, and Macy has agreed to do the photography for the event. She aims to get a mix of nostalgic shots that will look great in the Mallory gallery online and some shots we can use for marketing purposes."

"And the finer details? Decorating, etcetera?"

Rhett waved a hand. "Everything is under control. My shipments have been on time so far, and everything is going according to schedule."

"Hiring you was a brilliant move." Cole locked the door to his office and Rhett set his tablet down on Cole's desk.

"It certainly was," Rhett agreed as Cole came up behind him and pressed their bodies together. Rhett had been concerned at first that there might be such a thing as too much togetherness. Cole responded to his concerns by assuring him that if he felt as if working together was too much, he'd still help Rhett launch his own business.

The opposite seemed to be true, and the more time they spent together, the closer Rhett felt to Cole. It had happened a while ago now, maybe on a dance floor in Tahiti, or maybe since then on one of their slow strolls through the vineyard. Rhett smiled, turning in Cole's arms, thinking about how Cole now remembered to stop and smell the grapes.

He hadn't told him yet, though. Sometimes Rhett thought the words would scare Cole away, and other times Rhett didn't tell him because there was no way Cole couldn't know how Rhett felt about him. He could swear there was a neon sign about his head that lit up and flashed the word *swoon* whenever he looked at Cole.

Rhett leaned in, pressing his mouth against Cole's, humming in approval. "Mmm. You taste like wine." He slid his hands up Cole's chest.

"I do run a vineyard." Cole responded, returning Rhett's exploratory kiss, his hands clutching at Rhett's waist.

Rhett didn't want to wait until they got home. He was greedy for Cole, for the feel of his skin against Rhett's and the sounds that only Cole could make. Rhett turned them, pressing the back of Cole's thighs against the desk.

"What are you doing?" Cole asked as he kissed his neck, his fingers working on the buttons of Cole's shirt.

"I'm going to fuck my boss. On his desk. In his office." Rhett pulled Cole's shirt loose and shoved it off his shoulders, kissing the now bare expanse of chest he loved so much. Cole leaned back, bracing his hands on his desk, a cup of pens clattering to the side and spilling onto the floor. Rhett laughed, flicking his tongue over Cole's nipple. "You're already making a mess and I haven't even started yet."

Cole's fingers danced along Rhett's scalp, wrapping around his hair, gripping a handful. He turned Rhett's head, commanding that Rhett look at him. Rhett gave him what he wanted, what his parted lips begged for, and he met Cole's mouth, licking his way inside as he fumbled with Cole's button.

When the stubborn button popped free, he tugged at Cole's pants, easing them down to his knees. Rhett wrapped his fingers around the back of Cole's head and locked him into a blistering kiss, then he pulled away suddenly and sank to his knees.

He watched Cole's head tilt back and he practically felt the groan that rumbled out of him when he took Cole's cock into his mouth. He ran his hands up Cole's thighs, enjoying the feeling of firm flesh beneath his fingers. He loved the way Cole was slightly hairy on his chest and all down his legs. He pulled himself away from Cole's cock and took his balls into his mouth next, laving his tongue over the soft flesh, ignoring the way his own cock pressed uncomfortably hard against the zipper of his pants.

"Rhett, fuck." Cole sounded the best when he was on the verge of losing his mind, Rhett thought. When his voice reached a certain breathless pitch, it delighted Rhett to get him there, then pound him into oblivion and keep him there for as long as possible.

"Something you want, baby?" Rhett asked, slipping a finger into his mouth and wetting it with his saliva, then pressing it against Cole's hole, grinning wickedly at the groan it elicited.

"That. I want that," Cole answered quickly, his ass doing a lovely job of taking Rhett's finger.

He wrapped his lips around Cole's cock and slowly sucked him down to the root, his finger stroking in and out, twisting, loosening Cole for him. Above him, Cole gripped the edge of the desk and panted, peppering his staccato breaths with expletives and Rhett's name. Always Rhett's name. His name, Rhett discovered, meant many things to Cole depending on how he said it.

Rhett. More. Rhett. Faster. Rhett. Please. Rhett. Harder. Rhett. I need you. Rhett. Rhett. Rhett. Rhett. Rhett. Which seemed to mean that Cole's mind was blown and the only thing he knew in that moment was Rhett.

Rhett stood and slammed his mouth down on Cole's, tasting him, full bodied like a wine and twice as appealing, getting him just as drunk. Cole reached for him, untucking his shirt and making quick work of undoing his pants and pulling Rhett's cock out.

Rhett broke the kiss and turned Cole around, pressing his torso down against the desk. He left him there for a moment and fumbled into one of the drawers to get the lube Cole had begun keeping there since Rhett started working with him.

He slicked his cock and returned to Cole, running a hand down his spine, watching the way his hand looked so perfect against Cole's skin.

"Don't wait." Cole pleaded, his eyes mirroring the inferno that burned out of control inside Rhett.

Rhett lined up at Cole's entrance and pushed inside in one long slow glide of skin and skin and nothing in between them. It had been that way for months now; each of them giving the other something they'd never given any other person before—their complete trust.

He laid himself over Cole, running his hands up Cole's arms until their fingers tangled. He sucked and kissed between his shoulders, down his neck, leaving a litany of marks there, showing anyone and everyone who might see them that Cole belonged to Rhett. It was territorial as all hell, but Cole was Rhett's. He hadn't had the guts yet to say the words, but Rhett knew he loved Cole.

He pressed a kiss between Cole's shoulder blades and breathed his name against his skin, breathing the truth instead of saying it aloud, as his hips snapped and his cock slid in and out of Cole's gorgeous ass. Pressing his forehead against Cole's back, he slowed his frantic pace and brought Cole down from the edge.

"Rhett, please." Cole's voice was a combination of frustration and satisfaction that Rhett loved hearing.

"Please what, baby? What do you need?" Rhett teased, only moving slightly now, grinning when Cole rocked his ass back to fuck himself on Rhett's cock.

"You. Please. I need you," Cole whined.

Rhett stood up. Releasing Cole's hands, he gripped his hips instead. Slamming back into Cole as hard as he could, he closed his eyes, dangerously close to losing himself. He pressed a hand between Cole's shoulders, pinning him to the desk. His other hand gripped Cole's hip, likely leaving bruises, as he pounded into him.

Electric pleasure shot through every nerve in Rhett's body, pushing him to thrust faster, fuck harder, go deeper. Underneath him, Cole stared up at Rhett, his face plastered to the desk, his eyes hooded and glassy. Even as they fell apart, coming in hoarse shouts and frantic whimpers, they were unable to look away from each other.

Rhett's cock twitched and pulsed as Cole's ass spasmed and he pulled Cole up, kissing him, before sliding out and letting Cole take over, spinning around and claiming Rhett's mouth, his fingers buried in Rhett's hair.

Rhett pulled away; grinning at Cole, he leaned in and stole a kiss. "You made a mess." Rhett remarked, referring to the pools of cum on Cole's desk.

"Mmm. I did, did I?" Cole kissed the corner of his mouth, his hands groping Rhett's ass, grinding their half-hard cocks together, not caring if he was messing up Rhett's clothing. It was the end of the day and home was their next stop. "You should clean it up for me."

Rhett reached for the tissue, but Cole grabbed his hand and brought Rhett's knuckles to his lips. "With your mouth, baby."

Rhett arched an eyebrow, then turned to the desk and bent over. He stuck his tongue out and licked the mess Cole made off the wood being careful not to swallow once he got it all. He stood and pulled Cole into a kiss, letting him share his release.

Cole pulled away and tugged his pants up. "When we get home, baby, you're in so much trouble."

Rhett tucked himself back into his pants. "You say the nicest things." Rhett kissed him again, unable to keep himself from tasting him.

"I only say things I mean, baby. Remember that."

Chapter Twenty-Seven
COLE

It was just before noon when Rhett walked out the door, camera around his neck and notebook tucked under his arm. He was off to meet with Macy for a wedding that was scheduled for sunset at the vineyard. What sort of person decided to get married the weekend before Christmas, Cole thought, strolling through the expansive front part of the house toward the kitchen in the back.

Lucy, Rhett's fern, sat happily on the windowsill over the sink, and Cole scoffed at himself. How could a plant be happy? Or sad, for that matter. It was a plant. Whether it had a name or not. Lucy was a fern.

Cole cast a sidelong glance to the corner of his dining room where the remaining boxes of leftover Christmas decorations were stacked. A few days earlier, he and Rhett had bought a Christmas tree, fit it into the corner of the living room near the fireplace and set to decorating it.

They'd spent hours together, going through Cole's family ornaments, ones that had been passed down to him from his parents and grandparents, and ones he'd picked up along the way on his own. Rhett had darted out to the garage, returning with an armful of tissue paper wrapped baubles that they carefully opened and added to the tree.

The decorations were a mashup of classic ball ornaments and mismatched heirlooms. Their tree, with its colors and clear twinkle lights, made Cole smile every time he looked at it.

He carefully picked Lucy up from the windowsill, tucked her under his arm, and walked her to the living room, kicking one of the cardboard boxes of leftover lights in front of him. Cole cleared a place for Lucy on the mantle and set her down, fluffing her leaves with his fingers. He squatted on the ground and opened the box, digging around until he found a small string of battery-operated lights.

Cole had another box in his pocket, a small, velvet one, that he removed and set on the mantle beside Lucy's black pot. He patted the top of the box then turned his attention back to the fern, carefully stringing the lights between her leaves.

"It's time we had a talk, Lucy," he told the fern, conversationally.

Cole flipped the small switch on the battery box at the end of the light string and they lit up, illuminating Lucy so she matched the tree. Cole chuckled, wondering why Rhett hadn't thought to name the tree itself. He picked the velvet box up again and flipped the lid open, displaying the contents to the plant.

"Lucy, I want to marry your dad. I hope that's okay."

Cole turned the box around so he could see its contents and he fingered the thin white gold band that sat nestled inside. He'd known when he saw it, inlaid with a delicate looking vine filigree, that it was perfect for Rhett. He hoped Lucy would approve of the acknowledgement.

He had agreed months ago that he would give Rhett the proposal he wanted, with the Santa hats and the Christmas lights, but ring specifications weren't something they'd ever discussed. He traced his thumb over the vines and leaves that looped the ring and smiled, thinking how perfect it would look against Rhett's skin.

The past months had been...spectacular, his fascination with Rhett not even close to waning. Bringing Rhett on at the vineyard had been a wise business decision. Rhett was working with Elena toward the launch of Mallory Bubbly Wines on New Year's Eve, and as an added bonus, Cole got to fuck on his lunch break at least once a week. He was nearly obsessed with Rhett, eager and ready to explore every inch of him from his skin to his soul.

Cole tucked the ring back into the box and snapped it closed, sliding it into his pocket. He patted it, just to make sure it was safe. His phone vibrated in his other pocket and he pulled it out, seeing a text from Ryan.

Ryan: Open up, bitch.

Cole shoved the phone back in his pocket and opened the front door, revealing his best friend standing on his porch with a pizza in his hands.

"You know pizza doesn't go with mulled wine, right?" Cole laughed, letting him inside.

"Pizza goes with everything," Ryan argued, kicking the door closed behind him.

"No, wine goes with everything," Cole countered, trailing Ryan into the dining room.

"Where's my brother?" he asked, trying to look around the house as casually as he could manage.

"At work with Macy."

"Why is he still doing work with her?" Ryan asked, flipping the box open. "Are you not fulfilling him during the day?"

Cole scrunched his nose. "Is that where we are now? Making innuendos about whether I can sexually satisfy your brother?"

Ryan mimicked Cole's face then stuck his tongue out in disgust. "You're a pervert. I meant career-wise. Jesus, Cole, I don't even know why I'm friends with you sometimes."

"You're friends with me because I'm the coolest person you know," Cole reminded him, biting into a slice of pizza.

"I'm friends with you because you own a never ending supply

of alcohol," Ryan countered, reaching across the table for the thermos of mulled wine Cole had set out earlier.

"I don't own it."

"Yet."

"Yet," Cole agreed.

Fact of the matter was, Kristen was due back from her honeymoon in a couple days and the whole family was going to do Christmas Day together at Cole's parents' house. He was hopeful he'd hear news about the ownership transfer soon, especially since his parents had brought it up to begin with back in the fall. He also anticipated his sister returning from her world traveling pregnant, ever intent on being the center of attention.

"So," Cole asked, wiping his hands on his jeans, "you're coming to the bubbly launch, right?"

"Rhett would murder me if I didn't," Ryan answered with a laugh.

Cole smiled. "He's been working really hard on the whole thing. He wants it all to be perfect. He's doing math? I don't know, like trying to calculate how many bottles we need available for the toast and the casual drinking, and he's just really into the whole thing."

"Three point four glasses, plus toast," Ryan remarked, an eerie echo from the number Rhett had been rambling about in the days prior.

"Has he been talking your ear off about it, too?"

"No." Ryan finished his first slice of pizza and washed it down with a large swallow of wine. "It's some calculation he came up with when we were in college, trying to help plan the frat liquor purchases more cost effectively."

"That is...." Cole trailed off, shaking his head, "very much Rhett."

Rhett's little idiosyncrasies had grown on Cole over the time they'd lived together, from his meticulous food measuring on the times that Cole had let him cook dinner, to things like the drink per person average that he'd apparently been fine-tuning since college.

Every day there was something new, something more about Rhett that served to remind Cole he was the luckiest man on the planet. And lucky in more ways than one. What if Rhett hadn't been the one to stumble into him at Tubby's when he had? What if Cole had done something ridiculous like try to fake-marry Ryan, or worse, a stranger?

Cole glanced behind him at Lucy, sitting proud and twinkling on the mantle as if she'd belonged there all along.

"I need to tell you something," Cole blurted, turning his attention back to Ryan, who poured himself a second mug of mulled wine.

Cole snagged it from his hand and took a drink, the warmth of cloves and cinnamon settling against his tongue. Ryan snatched it back and grumbled about Cole needing to get his own.

"What?" Ryan asked, mouth full of another bite of pizza.

"Just, uh, wait a second," Cole said, scratching the top of his lip. He hopped up and jogged to the front door, pulling it open just before Penny was able to knock.

"Cole," she greeted with a warm smile and a baby strapped to her chest.

"Thanks for coming," he said with a smile, letting her inside.

"Of course," she said, pulling her jacket off and tossing it on the side table.

Cole looked down at Tyson, who was sound asleep, head at what Cole assumed had to be a terribly painful angle. "Doesn't that hurt?"

"Oh, no," she said with a quiet laugh. "Their bones are like jelly at this age."

"Where's David?" Cole asked, leading Penny through the house.

"Oh, he's sleeping."

"That's nice of you to not wake him up and leave Tyson at home," Cole laughed. "Do you want some pizza?"

"Yeah, but, oh, is that wine?" she sniffed the air and gestured toward the mug and thermos in front of Ryan.

"It is. Let me get you a glass." Cole walked into the kitchen, getting a mug for him and another for Penny.

"How's the wee lad?" Ryan asked, stroking his hand down the outside of the baby carrier without touching Tyson.

"Are you Scottish now?" Penny scoffed, taking Ryan's wine and making it her own. Cole slid one of the empty mugs toward Ryan, who filled them both.

"Is your son a brand of chicken?" Ryan asked, pursing his lips and shaking his head.

"You're a dick. I wish Rhett could disown you," Penny snarked.

"You definitely don't wish that at all. You love me."

"I know," Penny agreed, lifting the mug above Tyson's head and taking a sip. "This is divine, Cole."

"Thanks," Cole replied, a prideful blush coloring his cheeks.

"Speaking of delicious Mallory vintages, how excited is Rhett about the bubbly launch?" Penny grinned, setting the mug down and grabbing a slice of pizza, maneuvering it carefully over Tyson's head and taking a bite.

"Terribly excited in his normal calculated way," Cole answered, taking a deep breath. "But that's not what I invited you guys over for."

"Yeah, I noticed," Ryan said, his eyes narrowing in accusation. "What did you have to say? Are you and Rhett breaking up or something? Because I just got used to this and I don't want things to be weird again."

"No!" Cole waved his hands in front of him in a denial. "We're not breaking up. Actually, I just...God, this is nerve-wracking. I'm going to ask him to marry me."

"What?" Ryan barked out, choking on a pepperoni that he quickly washed down with a gulp of wine.

Penny squinted and bit her lips between her teeth. She stroked a free hand over Tyson's tuft of hair and sniffled.

"I'm going to propose to Rhett. On Christmas Eve." Cole dug

the ring box out of his pocket and slid it across the table toward where Penny and Ryan sat.

"You son of a bitch," Ryan said, though not angrily. "With the Santa hats?"

"How did you know about the Santa hats?" Cole asked in shock.

Penny reached for the ring box and flipped the lid open, sucking in a pleased breath when she saw the ring he'd bought for Rhett. There was an identical one upstairs for himself, assuming everything went as planned when he popped the question.

"Oh, Cole," she murmured, tracing the vine detail on the ring. She looked up at him and smiled. "Everyone knows about the Santa hats."

"Rhett has dreamed about his Christmas proposal since he was a kid," Ryan answered. "He used to watch those sappy movies with Mom before she died."

Cole swallowed, making a note of that very important detail that Rhett had neglected to tell him about.

"You're sure about this?" Penny asked, snapping the box closed and dropping it back onto the table. "You haven't been together that long. It seems so soon."

"I know," Cole agreed, his voice thick with emotion and unspoken love, "and this isn't what either of us intended when we got involved with each other, but now I can't imagine it being any other way."

Chapter Twenty-Eight
RHETT

Rhett smiled at Lucy sitting on the mantle in the living room, sporting a set of twinkle lights of her very own. They were tiny battery-operated ones and when Rhett asked Cole about them, he'd smiled and explained that Lucy was jealous of the tree. It was ridiculous, but that's why Rhett loved Cole.

He'd held onto that knowledge, though, keeping it close to his chest. It was Christmas Eve and they'd discussed getting engaged today to try and win Cole's grandparents over to the idea of giving the vineyard to him. The very thought that Cole had to do something so 1800s, like get a spouse to prove his worth or that he was responsible enough, rankled Rhett. He'd do anything to help him make it happen, even get fake-engaged to his very real boyfriend.

But since Rhett moved in, Cole hadn't mentioned the proposal or the engagement, so while part of Rhett was certain it would happen, another part of him was positive that it wouldn't. Either way, Rhett tried not to think about it. They'd had a lovely Christmas Eve so far. They slept in, then spent the morning taking a stroll through the vineyard. Cole insisted on taking him to lunch and they chose a quiet place across town.

"I need the washroom," Rhett said, getting to his feet. "Can you order for me if the waitress comes?" He had wanted to cook for Cole, but he pleaded with Rhett, pinning him down on the couch and peppering him with kisses, tickling his ribs until he agreed to let Cole take him out for an early dinner.

"Sure thing, baby." Cole blew him a kiss, which Rhett did not pretend to catch.

When he returned a few minutes later, his drink had been refreshed so he guessed that he'd missed the waitress. "What did you order me?"

"Macaroni and cheese with a garden salad." Cole took a sip of his drink. "Did you have a nice lunch with Penny yesterday?"

Rhett loved that Cole got along well with his best friend; he even seemed to like little Tyson.

"Oh, my God, Penny told me that David is trying to convince her to have another baby."

"Tyson's what, nine months?"

"Eight. He still hasn't been out longer than he was in and David wants another."

"Insanity."

"She told him if he wanted another right now..." Rhett grabbed his glass and took a sip. "That he'd have to carry it himself."

"Would you want kids?" Cole asked. Rhett supposed that the question wasn't out of nowhere. They were currently talking about children, it was probably the natural progression of the conversation, yet Rhett blushed.

"I wouldn't mind. Not right now, but maybe down the road."

"Surrogate or adoption?"

"Either one, both maybe. I haven't put that much thought into it." Rhett shrugged a shoulder.

"Liar." Cole grinned. "You think about everything you do. I think I'd want to adopt," Cole admitted. "Though the idea of having little Rhetts running around isn't unappealing. Twins would be neat."

They talked and laughed until their lunch arrived and Rhett looked at Cole's BLT longingly. His macaroni and cheese didn't look terrible, but it didn't look like a bacon-loaded sandwich either. He lifted a forkful to his mouth and took a bite. The texture was weird, sort of mushier than he'd expected and the cheese tasted funny, not quite cheese-like. Rhett had an inkling about what happened and decided to turn the tables on Cole.

"Oh, my God, Cole," he moaned. "This is amazing!" Rhett took another bite, chewing and swallowing, devouring the noodles. "You have to try it." He loaded his fork and held it out for Cole. "It's delicious."

Cole looked skeptical, but leaned forward and dutifully ate the offered bite. Rhett watched his face contort as he reached for his napkin. "That's disgusting," Cole complained, careful to keep his voice down.

"Did you seriously order me vegan macaroni and cheese? But more, did you think I wouldn't notice?"

Cole took a huge sip of his drink. "You started it."

"That's just mean. You're lucky I adore you."

Cole wiped his tongue with his napkin. "You're lucky you're not really vegan."

The practical joke took Rhett's mind off the looming proposal, which may or may not happen. If it didn't happen, he still wasn't sure whether to be disappointed or relieved. If it was fake, at least he got his dream proposal. But to have it be real...Rhett couldn't entertain the idea because he wanted it too much.

<hr>

They spent the afternoon at home together, wrapping presents and reminiscing about past Christmases. After they wrapped gifts for Tyson, laughing at how spoiled kids nowadays were, they ate a lovely Christmas Eve dinner that, thankfully, was not vegan macaroni and cheese. For dinner, Cole had cooked shrimp, and fish, and crab, an imitation of the dish they'd eaten at that out of the way restaurant in Tahiti. After dinner, Cole took Rhett's hands and tugged him into the living room.

"It's time to exchange presents," Cole said, taking a seat on the floor in front of the tree. There were only two boxes for them under the tree, and to Rhett's dismay, the box containing his present was far too large to be an engagement ring. It was just as well, Rhett thought, there were no Santa hats anyway. It wouldn't be his dream proposal otherwise.

"Open yours first." Rhett said, grabbing the box and handing it to Cole. His hands trembled a little and he felt suddenly ridiculous about his gift.

Cole pulled the ribbon off the box and gently removed the lid. The smile on his face made Rhett feel a little better about his gift. "His name is Ricky," Rhett said. "I figured he'd look nice next to Lucy. Or you could take him to your office."

Cole held the tiny potted fern with great care, his fingers brushing the delicate leaves. "I love him. He's perfect." Cole set him aside and leaned forward to steal a kiss from Rhett. "Your turn." Cole said, his mouth still kissably close.

Cole reached under the tree and handed Rhett his gift. He tore into the paper, suddenly eager to see what was inside. Rhett opened the flaps of the box and removed the tissue paper.

He looked at Cole. "Santa hats," he said, scarcely able to breathe. "You got me Santa hats."

"Put one on," Cole said, taking the other from the box and putting it on. Rhett followed his example, and somehow, with his jittery fingers, he managed to get the hat on. "Now keep digging."

Rhett turned his attention back to the box and dug in more tissue paper until he saw it. "Oh, my God, Cole. How?" Rhett asked, dumbfounded as he saw the same pot he'd fallen in love with in Tahiti.

"Getting it was the easy part. Waiting for Christmas to give it to you? That was the hard part." Cole grinned and leaned back. "Go slip her into her new dress. I bet she'll love it."

Rhett stood and took the pot over to Lucy. Her current pot was a cheap plastic one that'd he'd transplanted her into and it fit in the new pot with room to spare. "I think she looks lovely. I can't believe you got it for me." He stroked his finger along the edge of the pot. "Thank you."

Rhett turned and there, kneeling in front of him and the tree, under the lights and in a Santa hat, just like in all his fantasies, was Cole. Cole was the newest addition to the fantasy, but he was the best part of it. Better than the Santa hats or the sound of carols softly playing in the background. Better than the perfectly lit tree, a mishmash of their ornaments, even better than Lucy on the mantle in a set of lights.

"Rhett," Cole said, his voice trembling more than it did in Rhett's imagination. "A few months ago, we both got this crazy idea that we could fake being together, that somehow we could fool everyone into thinking we were a couple and that we could do it without our own feelings getting tangled up." Cole swallowed and Rhett shook. He stood frozen, as Cole opened a ring box that Rhett hadn't noticed until that very moment.

"Cole," Rhett started to talk, but Cole took his hand and shushed him.

"Rhett, the only people we fooled were ourselves. This might have started off as a farce, but it's the most real thing in my life. *You* are the most real thing in my life. How I spent my whole life standing next to you, but not beside you, is a mystery to me. Rhett, I want to marry you. I want to marry you for real. I want to stand beside you, with you, for the rest of my life. I love you." Cole took a deep breath and gripped Rhett's hand tighter. "Rhett Alexander Kingston, will you marry me?"

"Cole," Rhett exhaled, his entire body trembling. "Before I answer, you need to know something." He took a deep breath. "I love you, too. I've loved you since that night in Tahiti."

"Which night?" Cole grinned, his relief palpable, his smile suddenly broader.

"All of them." Rhett admitted. "All of them, Cole. It's been real for me for a long time."

"Then marry me."

"Yes, Cole, yes. I'll marry you."

Cole pulled Rhett down to him and captured his mouth in a brutal kiss, their teeth clacking as they both broke out in laughter, stopping only to slip the rings on each other's fingers. Cole leaned against the couch, pulling Rhett into his arms.

"When was it real for you?" He looked up at Cole, suddenly eager to know.

"I don't know that it was ever truly just pretend for me," Cole admitted, "Once the idea of you became a reality, I couldn't stop wanting you. I wanted to know you and all your secrets. I wanted to know how you like your coffee and what you wear to bed at night. But if you want an actual, precise moment," Cole gazed at the tree for a minute and Rhett watched the way Cole smiled at whatever memory he was playing in his head.

Cole looked back at him. "Definitely in Tahiti, when I woke up next to you that first time."

Rhett laughed. "When I launched myself onto the floor?"

Cole smiled at him and chuckled before answering. "I woke up next to you knowing that I never wanted to wake up anywhere else ever again."

Chapter Twenty-Nine
COLE

"Don't be nervous," Cole whispered, adjusting the Santa hat on Rhett's head before ringing the doorbell at his parents' house.

"Easy for you to say," Rhett hissed out, his arms stacked full of wrapped gift boxes.

"Cole," his mother greeted warmly, pulling the door open and offering him a hug.

"Mom," he replied.

"Merry Christmas, Mrs. Mallory," Rhett said from behind his shield of gifts.

"Please, dear. Constance," she reminded him before calling over her shoulder. "Malcom, come help with these boxes."

Cole's father appeared, a broad smile across his face, and he helped Rhett inside, pulling the top three boxes from the stack.

"Merry Christmas, boys."

"Merry Christmas, Mr. Mallory," Rhett replied.

Cole's dad shot Rhett a sharp look before leading him into the house. Rhett looked over his shoulder helplessly at Cole, who just smiled and waved him off.

"I have some news, Mom," Cole whispered to his mother at the same time she said to him, "Your sister has some news."

Cole rolled his eyes. "I'm sure I know what Kristen has to say."

He experienced a moment of rage when he thought about how this morning wasn't just another moment where Kristen would steal his spotlight, but now it was Rhett's spotlight too. Getting engaged was a big deal and it didn't deserve anyone's half attention.

"Be nice," his mother warned, pushing him backward onto one of the loveseats. Cole watched Rhett arrange presents around the tree with his father, then he scanned the room. Kristen and Edward were snuggled together in front of the fire, of course in the center of the room. His parents were on the large sofa that lined a side wall and his grandparents in matching chairs between Cole and his parents.

On the coffee table in the middle of the room sat a spread of breakfast treats, from muffins to pastries, and a small platter of eggs and bacon. Rhett stood from the tree and laughed at something Cole's father said before turning to join Cole on the couch.

He stopped and pointed down at the table, and Cole nodded. Rhett picked up the carafe of coffee and poured two mugs, one for each of them, then snatched a muffin and returned to Cole.

"This couch is ridiculous," Rhett whispered as he fell into the cushions.

"I know," Cole agreed, bringing the mug to his lips and taking a small sip.

"Now that everyone is here," Kristen announced, "Edward and I have some news."

"Merry Christmas, Kristen," Cole interrupted, a bit dryly. "I have some news, too."

Kristen's nostrils flared, but years of practiced training of how to act in front of her elders quickly took over and she forced a polite smile.

"Merry Christmas, Cole." Her eyes shifted to Rhett and scanned him from shoes to hair. "Rhett."

"Kristen," Rhett greeted, with what Cole had come to know as Rhett's phone voice. The one he specifically reserved for dealing with vendors who were jerking him around on pricing or deadlines.

Cole reached for Rhett's hand and twined their fingers together, pressing a quick kiss to his knuckles.

"Do you mind?" Cole asked politely. Kristen narrowed her eyes at him in the quickest flash, then gestured with her hand.

"Of course not, Cole. It can be a day for good news all around." She smiled at him and it was so saccharine it made Cole's teeth hurt.

He looked at Rhett, whose eyes shone like the lights that were wrapped around their tree at home. He couldn't stop himself from thinking about how crazy the past few months had been. From his desperation at the thought of losing the vineyard, to the wild idea he and Rhett hatched at Tubby's, to now with things between them as real and tangible as the gold bands on their hands.

He smiled at Rhett and squeezed his hand. "I love you."

"I love you, Mr. Mallory."

"Well, don't keep us in suspense," Kristen bit out icily.

Cole took a deep breath.

"Rhett and I are getting married," he announced.

Kristen's face twitched and she managed a congratulatory smile. "That's amazing news, Cole. I know we were all starting to wonder if it was ever going to happen."

Cole's mother laughed and his father relaxed into the couch, like he'd been holding his breath for years and was finally able to let it out.

"That's wonderful," Constance said, using her husband's leg to push herself up from the couch. She closed the space between them and held her arms open. Cole stood, taking Rhett with him, and his mother wrapped her arms around them both.

"I'm proud of you," she whispered into Cole's ear.

Rhett's muscles unwound and Cole squeezed his shoulder. His mother pulled back and held her hand out.

"Now let me see the ring."

Rhett held his hand out awkwardly and Cole's mother examined the fine gold band around his finger, holding it up to the flickering light from the fireplace and sending an appreciative glance in Cole's direction.

"That's lovely," she announced. "I'm so excited for both of you. Isn't this exciting, Malcom?"

His father recognized the polite warning in her voice and he stood up, joining them in the center of the room. He shook Cole and Rhett's hands before leading Constance back to the couch. Cole swallowed and sat back down, trying to focus on Rhett's broad smile instead of his grandparents' noticeable silence.

"Thanks, Kris," Cole told his sister thankfully. "Now what's your news?"

He placed Rhett's hand on his knee and covered it with his own, his palms damp with nervous sweat. He already knew what Kristen's news was, but the longer the silence from the corner of the room went on, the more worried he became.

"It's much sooner than we'd planned, but Edward and I are pregnant!" Kristen exclaimed, projecting a bright smile across the room to their grandparents. Edward looked...surprisingly miserable, considering he was a newlywed, but he unwrapped himself from Kristen's entanglement to meet Cole's father near the table for a hug.

"How lovely," his mother enthused, "I get a new son and a grandbaby in the same day. It's my turn to be Nan."

Cole's actual Nan huffed an incredulous sound from the chair she was perched in, then reached across and swatted at her husband.

"What?" he asked, as though he hadn't been present in the room for the two life-changing announcements that his grandchildren had just shared.

"Kristen is pregnant," she told him, wagging a bony finger toward the fireplace.

"And Cole is getting married," his mother reminded her softly.

"Right. A baby," Jacob said, reaching into his jacket pocket.

Cole's blood turned to ice. He could feel Rhett's eyes on him, but he couldn't manage the strength to meet his stare.

Cole watched as his grandfather handed his Nan a thick, white envelope. He knew what it was. He knew what was happening.

This was such a surreal moment, maybe even more so than when he'd realized for the first time that he loved Rhett. His head spun and it was like he wasn't present in the room; he was just a helpless bystander, about to watch his life unravel before him.

"Cole." Rhett's worried voice in his ear wasn't enough to anchor him in the present.

He watched in carefully controlled horror as his Nan passed the envelope that held his life's work across the room to his sister.

"In light of your recent marriage and now the baby, your grandfather and I have drawn up the paperwork to have Mallory Vineyard transferred into your name."

From across the room, Constance throttled back a choking sound, and Cole closed his eyes before Kristen's fingers connected with the proffered envelope.

"Oh, that's incredibly generous of you, Mrs. Mallory," Edward said.

Cole heard shuffling around the room, but he remained frozen in place. He was scared if he opened his eyes, the room would literally be upside down. He swallowed back his tears and forced his eyes open.

"Look at me," Rhett's voice was low and hushed against his ear.

Cole turned to his fiancé, needing to pull his lips between his teeth to stop himself from breaking down completely when he saw the look of pity and concern on Rhett's face.

"It's fine," Rhett whispered and Cole jerked his head to the side.

"It's not," he countered, voice hushed. "I made you promises."

Cole grabbed for Rhett's hand, the cool metal of the band around his finger the only thing able to ground Cole in the present.

"All I want is you," Rhett promised, pressing a soft kiss against the corner of Cole's mouth before turning his attention to Kristen. "Congratulations, Kristen."

"Oh, thanks," she replied, casually, tossing the envelope onto the floor near the fire.

Cole sucked in a breath, and Edward picked up the envelope, tucking it into his jacket.

"Well," Constance started, taking stock of the room and making a quick retreat to the tree. "That was unexpected."

She laughed awkwardly and picked up two wrapped boxes. "Let's open gifts then, shall we?"

Cole's mother passed around the boxes that had been assembled under the tree, and Cole blindly went through the motions of unwrapping, and thanking, and saying you're welcome whenever appropriate. He'd never hated his life more than he did at that moment, and he hated that his first Christmas with Rhett had been ruined.

After what Cole hoped had been a satisfactory amount of time, he pushed away from the couch to stand.

"I think it's time for us to head home," he said curtly.

Rhett joined him, wrapping an arm around his waist. "You've all been so lovely. I appreciate being invited."

Cole gritted his teeth together, aware that Rhett was trying to save face for him and hating that he even had to.

"Oh, dear, you're part of the family now," Constance said, crossing toward them and hugging them separately.

"Cole, I'm sorry," she whispered into his ear. He believed her, and he patted her back in a conciliatory manner before stepping away without a reply.

He and Rhett gathered up their gifts and were halfway to the door before Edward's voice echoed down the hallway.

"Cole," he called.

Cole stopped and inhaled a sharp and shaking breath before turning around to face his brother-in-law.

"Yeah?"

"I'll have my people get in touch after the new year to discuss a transition plan for the vineyard. Sound good?"

Cole blinked, pivoting on his heel without saying a word. He pulled the front door open, the light of the day surprisingly bright and blinding. He shielded his eyes and followed Rhett to the car.

He drove them in silence back to their house, walking inside and leaving the presents in the trunk. He climbed the stairs to their bedroom, discarding his clothes as he went. By the time he reached the foot of the bed, he was naked, save for his engagement ring.

Rhett came before him, his head angled and he watched Cole with a look of uncertainty.

"I need you, please," Cole pleaded.

Rhett nodded, stripping down and then walking Cole backward onto the messy bed. They hadn't bothered to make it this morning. Rhett kicked the comforter out of their way and covered Cole's neck with kisses, peppering him with praise and promises that Cole didn't expect him to keep.

Cole offered himself to Rhett, silently, too wrapped up in his own painful need to verbalize what he wanted, what he needed, but he didn't have to. Rhett took him, slow at first, then fast, before slowing down again. Rhett drove Cole to the edge over, and over, and over, until the only thought left in Cole's mind was the only thought that mattered.

Rhett.

Chapter Thirty
RHETT

Cole sat on the floor in front of Rhett. Rhett massaged his shoulders and stared at the laptop as Cole typed away, hammering out last minute emails before the launch on New Year's Eve.

"I don't know why I'm bothering with any of this."

"Because you love the vineyard and you won't abandon her. I know this didn't go how we planned, Cole, but we'll get through it."

Cole scoffed and hit *send*, his finger aggressively stabbing at the laptop. "You're the only good thing that has come out of this." His voice quieted, "I feel like I've let you down."

Rhett leaned down, wrapping his arms around Cole's shoulders, and setting his chin on the top of his head. "You've done no such thing. You, Mr. Mallory, have exceeded all my expectations."

Cole turned his head and looked at him. The sadness in his eyes had lingered there since Christmas Day and there was a large part of Rhett that hated Cole's grandparents, and Kristen, who didn't even care about the vineyard. "I'll still do what I can to help you launch your business, Rhett. I can sell the house. It's in my name; they can't take it from me."

He put his hand over Cole's mouth. "You'll do no such thing.

We will figure this out, Cole. Maybe there's a way you can stay on at the vineyard."

Cole shook his head. "Edward said his people would be in touch with mine about the transition. It's a done deal. There's nothing I can do, Rhett." Cole turned back to the laptop and stared at the screen, then clicked over to the online checklist to check the status of some of the last minute tasks.

"Everything is on schedule, so far." Rhett explained, pointing at the screen. "The decorations go up tomorrow. I have to be there to oversee the flower delivery and get the caterers organized. Macy will be there two hours before the event starts to get some shots of the decor and the product. Elena will take over for me when I need to leave and get dressed."

"You're really good at this." Cole leaned over and kissed Rhett's forearm as he continued to point at things on the screen. "I--"

"Stop," Rhett cut him off. "If the next words out of your mouth are anything but *I can't wait to kiss my fiancé at midnight*, then I don't want to hear them." Rhett closed the laptop, then slid off the couch and onto the floor, wedging himself in behind Cole. "No more apologies. It's done and we did our best, and we'll do our best, and then we'll do our best somewhere else, together."

Cole leaned against Rhett, his head resting heavily on his shoulder. "I love this place. I love the vineyard. I love the grapes. I love the work," he said as he twisted around to look at Rhett, "but I love you more."

Rhett kissed the corner of Cole's mouth. "That's more like it." His heart ached for Cole and all that he'd lost. Cole spoke with his mother briefly the day after Christmas and she assured him that she'd done her best to reach out to his grandparents to change their minds, but it was already too late. The vineyard was Kristen's and Kristen was apparently refusing to talk about it. She'd waved her mother off with an airy sigh and called the whole ordeal bothersome.

"I have an idea," Rhett said suddenly, getting to his feet. "Stay there. Don't move."

He went to the kitchen and grabbed a bottle of their new sparkling wine, a couple of glasses, and a tray of cheese and meat from the fridge. He returned to the living room and set everything down on the coffee table. He turned the television off, which had been playing *I Love Lucy* reruns in the background all day.

"What are you doing?" Cole asked from his spot on the floor.

"One minute." Rhett grabbed a blanket off the couch and spread it out in front of the Christmas tree. He brought the wine and cheese over to the blanket then motioned for Cole to join him.

They sat cross-legged on the floor and Rhett poured them each a glass of wine.

"A few months ago, my only dream was to plan events. But then I met you, and you gave me a new dream." Rhett raised his glass and Cole gently clinked his against the side of it, the chime of glass kissing singing in the air. "To us."

"To us," Cole repeated, taking a drink.

"We could go anywhere. Do anything. We could move to New York and work on Broadway."

Cole snorted. "We really couldn't do that."

Rhett grinned and shrugged a shoulder. "We could. We can do anything. That's the rules tonight. Nothing is too outrageous. Nothing is out of our reach. If you could do anything, what would it be?"

Cole thought for a minute. "I'd be a beekeeper. I'd make flavored honey." His face took on a mischievous expression and he reached for a slice of cheese. "I'd make you my official honey tester. I bet you'd taste good drizzled in honey." Cole picked up a slice of cheese and fed Rhett from his fingers. "Your turn. What would you do?"

Rhett ate the cheese and took that time to consider his options. "I'd travel the world as a professional ping pong player. Or maybe I'd go to Japan and work in a cat café."

"We could open one here. Fill it with old, fat, shelter cats."

"We could make Ryan work there on weekends so we could sleep in."

Cole clinked their glasses together again. "I like the way you think. I bet Tyson would love it there."

"Penny wouldn't, she's allergic."

"Hmn, so maybe no cat café. We want something where our family can visit us."

Rhett slid closer to Cole. "Aww, you called her family." He only needed to sort of pretend that he was choked up. The reality was that it meant the world to him that Cole treated the things and the people that were precious to Rhett as also being precious to him. Rhett leaned in and pressed his lips against Cole's. "We'd run a vineyard," Rhett whispered against Cole's mouth. "We'd run a vineyard and you'd make wine and I'd plan parties and we would live happily ever after."

"It's the perfect end to a perfect story." Cole agreed, deepening the kiss. He pulled away, then moved the wine glasses and the cheese plate aside and kissed Rhett again, pressing him down into the blanket, smothering him with his weight, doing nothing more than kissing him and holding him.

"Walk with me." Cole whispered breathlessly against Rhett's cheek. Rhett agreed, and they stood, straightening their rumpled clothing. Cole grabbed the bottle of wine and they headed out into the backyard.

Though not part of the event tomorrow night, Rhett hadn't been able to resist decorating Cole's portion of the vineyard with twinkle lights. Rhett smiled and squeezed Cole's hand. "Did you know that my mom always wanted to see the entire vineyard lit up with twinkle lights?"

"No." Cole answered, taking a sip of wine from the bottle, then passing it off to Rhett. "Is that where your obsession with them comes from?"

"A little, I suppose. They're so...glamorous isn't really the way to describe them," Rhett chewed on his lower lip.

"Ethereal," Cole offered. "They transform the mundane into

something magical."

Rhett took a sip of wine to quench the heat inside of him. "Yeah. That's it exactly."

"She'd be proud of you, you know." Cole said, holding Rhett's hand a little tighter. "She'd like the person you became."

"She'd like you, too," Rhett offered Cole the wine.

Cole took it and gave him an odd look. "Do you think drinking wine in front of the grapes is appropriate? It's like drinking the blood of their dead in front of them."

"I'm fairly certain that they don't know. Plants don't really understand, Cole."

"You'd never say that about Lucy or Ricky." Cole shot back, tipping the wine up and taking another drink.

"They're not just plants. They're special."

"Maybe the grapes are special."

"Then no, baby, it's probably not appropriate to consume the dead in front of the living."

"Oops. Too late." Cole took another drink of wine then pulled Rhett in close to him. "Is it inappropriate to do this in front of the sentient grapes?" Cole asked before kissing Rhett, pulling their bodies together until no air or light could exist between them.

Rhett could still feel Cole the next morning when he crept downstairs and into the kitchen. Cole didn't need to be up for another hour, but Rhett wanted to get to the vineyard and make sure he was on top of things. He left a note for Cole, promising to be back in plenty of time to change into his tuxedo.

The event tonight had to be perfect, even though it was his first, and possibly his last ever at Mallory. He'd rather die than let Cole down. The vineyard was everything to Cole, and though he'd lost it, Rhett knew he still wanted to see it succeed.

He spent the morning arranging flowers, issuing orders, handling caterers, and a late shipment. He'd totally lost track of time when Macy and Elena showed up at the same time. Macy was dressed in an elegant pantsuit, her hair pinned up and out of her way while Elena was the opposite in a long flowing gown and hair cascading down her back to match.

"You," Elena said. "Get out of here. I have everything under control."

Rhett's stomach growled and he realized he hadn't eaten all day. "Okay," he said a little reluctantly. "But I'll have my phone on. Call or text if you need anything."

"I won't." Elena made a shooing motion even as Macy wandered around with her camera. "Get out of here."

Rhett went home, a little surprised to find Cole's car still in the driveway and when he walked into the house and smelled something delicious cooking, he was doubly confused. "Cole, baby? I'm back." Rhett called out, kicking his shoes off and heading to the kitchen.

"Hey, you." Cole tossed him a happy smile over his shoulder then went back to cooking. "I made us a quick dinner. It's going to be a long night. Elena told me that everything at the vineyard is ready."

Rhett sighed and rolled his shoulders. He was exhausted and the day was far from being over. "Everything is as ready as it's going to get. I have time for food, then to dress, and then we need to get up there."

Cole turned the stove off and grabbed a couple of plates from the cupboard. "Relax, baby," he said as he spooned some homemade macaroni and cheese onto a plate. Rhett must have looked at him funny because Cole grinned, handing him a plate and a fork. "It's not vegan, I promise."

"Good," Rhett said, taking his plate from Cole. "Because your boyfriend is not vegan."

"My *fiancé* is not vegan." Cole corrected. "But he is amazing."

"Mmm," Rhett hummed. "No, I think my fiancé is better than yours."

Cole leaned in and pressed his lips against Rhett's. "Them's fighting words."

"So fight me." Rhett shrugged and shoveled another bite of food into his mouth.

"Not tonight. Tonight, we dance."

"You look like you're in a better mood than you have been," Rhett observed.

"I am, because I have you and that's all that matters. My fiancé told me that."

"You're right," Rhett beamed. "Your fiancé is better than mine."

Chapter Thirty-One
COLE

Cole leaned against the bar, eyes surveying the extravagant event Rhett had managed to put together to celebrate the new year and the launch of Mallory Bubbly Wines. He sipped at his drink, the carbonation tickling his nose while he watched Rhett flit around, making sure everything was going smoothly.

"He's not going to be able to enjoy himself if you don't wrangle him," Penny laughed, coming to stand beside him. At the last minute, their sitter had fallen through and David had offered to stay home with Tyson so she could come support Rhett.

"He's not going to enjoy himself even if I do wrangle him because he'll be worrying about it."

"You're probably right," Penny agreed. She finished her glass of sparkling rosé and set it on the bar behind them.

"I want to dance," she groaned. "Do you think Ryan would dance with me?"

"I can't imagine he'd be able to turn you down," Cole said, leaning over and pressing a kiss against his rouged cheek.

She smiled and vanished, blending in to the crowd as she went to find Ryan, or some other unsuspecting victim, to dance with her. After watching Penny move around the dance floor, Cole reasoned David had probably been relieved when he found out he had to stay home with the baby.

Rhett really had done a magnificent job planning and assembling the launch party. The vineyard was transformed into something that looked like it was out of a movie. Cole chuckled to himself when he realized his fiancé had probably intentionally turned the vineyard into what could have easily doubled as the set of a Hallmark movie.

The mechanized back doors of the main building and tasting room were opened wide, pulled back allowing unhindered access from the inside to the vineyard. There was a huge black and white checkered dance floor that stretched from the building to a few feet shy of the vines.

Unsurprisingly, Rhett had hung clear bulb market lights in a crisscross pattern over the dance floor, lighting the vineyard up with a truly magical feel. Cocktail tables lined the dance floor and were decorated with elegant, yet simple floral centerpieces on top of vibrant, jewel-hued tablecloths.

Cole reached up and fingered his bow tie, a rich forest green color that Rhett had picked out for him. He was relieved to find he didn't match the tables, but looked like he'd matched the decor on purpose. Cole appreciated Rhett's small attempt to make him feel like he fit in at Mallory still, like he belonged, even though Cole knew he didn't. Not anymore.

His mother approached him, decked out in a sequined black cocktail dress that accentuated the green of her eyes.

"Mother," he greeted, leaning down and giving her a kiss.

Constance patted his arm fondly and turned with him to watch the hundreds of people dancing and laughing, but more importantly, drinking Mallory wine.

"How are you, darling?" she questioned.

Cole debated whether to give her the real answer, or the answer he'd been giving everyone the past week when they'd asked him the same question. He decided to lie, the irony of that like acid in his throat, but he wouldn't do anything to jeopardize the publicity that Rhett would get from a successful event tonight.

"I'm fine," he answered curtly.

"You lie," his mother countered.

Cole shrugged, grabbing a glass of wine off the tray of a passing waiter. "Rhett has put together a wonderful event for the vineyard and in the spring he's going to be my husband. There's nothing for me to complain about."

That, at least, was a half-truth. There was plenty for him to complain about.

"Cole," his mother soothed, but he raised a hand to stop her.

"Please, don't," he pleaded. "Not tonight. I want to have this. I want *him* to have this."

Cole took a long drink of his wine and gave his mother another kiss. "Enjoy your night, Mother."

Cole stepped away from the bar, putting as much distance between him and his mother as he could manage without looking like he was trying to escape. Once he was satisfied with the space between them, he stopped and checked his watch, pleased to find it was nearly midnight.

Penny's sharp laugh hit his ears and he looked up, finding Ryan obediently spinning her around the dance floor.

"That's nice of him," Rhett murmured, sliding his arms around Cole's waist and resting his cheek against his shoulder.

"Indeed," Cole agreed, covering one of Rhett's hands with his.

"Are you enjoying yourself?" Rhett asked, taking Cole's wine and drinking half the glass in one swallow.

Cole took the glass back. "I am. You've put together a perfect night, babe."

Rhett hummed in approval. "It'll be perfect when I get my midnight kiss."

"Ah, well, not too long then."

They stood in silence. Cole closed his eyes and absorbed his surroundings—the lights and sounds, the smell of the damp soil and grapes that most everyone overlooked, the warmth of Rhett's skin in the places they touched. As far as last memories went, this would be one worth keeping.

Without warning, the music went silent and the dance floor was flooded with shocked gasps, followed by silence. A microphone turned on and the speakers filled with feedback, then the familiar sound of Kristen's laughter.

"Oh, dear," she chuckled into the microphone.

Cole's head snapped toward the DJ booth and he found his sister on the stage, glass of what he hoped was cider in one hand and microphone in the other.

"What is she doing?" Rhett asked, voice laced with worry.

"I don't know," Cole answered, taking Rhett's hand and pushing his way through the crowd.

If looks could kill, he would have murdered Kristen where she stood.

"Has anyone seen my brother?" she asked, shielding her eyes from the lights and searching the crowd.

"What are you doing, Kristen?" he snapped, finally breaking through the throng of people and into her line of sight.

"Oh!" she exclaimed, "Here he is."

Rhett's palm was sweaty and sliding against Cole's and he did his best to maintain his grip, even as his heart rate skyrocketed.

"Kristen," he warned.

She shushed him with a careless wave of her glass in the air. Cole scrubbed his free hand over his face and waited for whatever attention grab she was going to pull now.

"For those of you who don't know, my name is Kristen Mallory. Well," she laughed, taking a drink of her beverage, "Kristen Mallory Fulton, since I'm married now, and my grandparents, Claire and Jacob Mallory own this vineyard."

There was a spattering of polite applause at the mention of his grandparents and he tried his best to not visibly bristle at the sound of their names.

"Well," Kristen said, for what Cole was certain was the twentieth time in her two minute speech, "actually, I own the vineyard."

There were a few audible gasps followed by some questionable applause. Cole took a step backward, ready to disappear into the crowd, hopeful the people would swallow him whole.

"I'm sorry," Rhett whispered, as though he was as devastated by Kristen's blatant announcement as he was.

"I want to leave," Cole answered softly, taking another step backward and bumping into Rhett's strong chest.

"There's going to be some changes after the new year," Kristen carried on, her voice more and more like nails on a chalkboard.

Cole closed his eyes.

"For those of you who don't know, my older brother Cole has been running Mallory for seven years. He graduated from college and came back to us here and has been making sure things ran smoothly ever since. This event was all him, and that delicious looking new bubbly wine."

Kristen stared longingly at her glass, and Cole was grateful to realize it really was only cider.

"It wasn't just me," Cole interrupted, his voice loud enough to draw his sister's attention. "I didn't do it alone. My fiancé, Rhett, he planned this entire event. The idea for Mallory Bubbly Wines is actually all his. And Elena Cordova, she did all the product development. And Laurence, too. He's the production manager."

Cole bit his tongue and tilted his head back, focusing on the lights strung above his head. Anything to stave off the wave of emotion that he was afraid of experiencing firsthand in front of this entire crowd of people.

"Right," Kristen agreed, casually. "And I don't even know who any of those people are."

"Jesus," Rhett hissed under his breath. Cole looked at Rhett, desperate to draw some strength or support from him before he climbed the stage and throttled his sister.

"That's why the idea of me inheriting Mallory Vineyard is preposterous," Kristen announced.

Cole choked, and angled a sharp look toward his sister. She set her glass down and wrapped all ten of her manicured nails around the microphone. She smiled at him, and it was an honest to goodness smile, not one of her put-on looks that she used when she was trying to impress someone.

"What?" he asked, though his voice was so soft he wasn't sure she heard him.

"I mean, don't get me wrong. I love this place. It's where I grew up, but Mallory is your *home,* Cole. I don't want to take that from you. And besides, I wouldn't even know what to do. It's not right for me to own this place and then pay you to do all the hard work."

"What are you saying?" he asked, fighting back a flicker of hope he thought long since snuffed out.

"You built this vineyard into what it is today, Cole. You deserve to own it, and I want you to have it."

Kristen reached over to one of the cocktail tables that had been set up near the DJ booth and picked up a recognizable white envelope, in addition to a larger manila envelope. She came to the edge of the stage and leaned down, offering both to him.

Rhett pushed him forward and he took the envelopes and clutched them to his chest like they were a long lost stuffed animal and he was a child, just reunited.

"But Edward said..." Cole trailed off, his fingers flexing around the thick paper he held.

Kristen covered the mic and rolled her eyes. "Edward has plenty of money."

She stood back up, elegant as ever, uncovering the microphone and speaking again, "There isn't a person on this planet who loves this vineyard more than my brother does, so I want him to have it. Come up here," she said, gesturing to the stage.

Cole looked to Rhett, whose eyes were glassy under the night sky, and he smiled, tipping his chin toward the stage. Cole climbed the steps, coming to stand beside his sister.

"I know it's almost midnight, so there's kissing and dancing, but I just want to make sure everyone here knows this face. My brother, Cole Mallory, the heart and soul, and new owner of Mallory Vineyards."

A raucous applause rang out through the vineyard and Cole grabbed Kristen, pulling her into a tight embrace.

"Thank you," he whispered into her ear.

"It was the easiest decision I ever made," Kristen told him, sincerely.

"We've got about fifteen seconds left, everyone," the DJ cut into announce. His baritone voice drew Cole back to reality and he looked down, seeing Rhett on the dance floor, waving his hands and encouraging Cole to return to him.

He jumped off the stage and jogged to Rhett, seizing him into his arms and holding their bodies together.

"Congratulations," Rhett whispered. "I'm so proud of you."

"Is this real?" Cole mumbled, as the crowd behind him counted down to five.

"It's about as real as our relationship is," Rhett answered with a teasing laugh.

"Oh," Cole agreed, "so it's really real."

"Really real," Rhett replied before lifting onto his toes and pressing his mouth against Cole's.

Cole parted his lips, letting Rhett inside, the taste of sauvignon grapes crisp on his tongue. Rhett held Cole's face in his hands and kissed him like he was air, through the New Year's Eve applause and through the off-key rendition of "Auld Lang Syne."

"I love you," Rhett murmured into his mouth, and Cole smiled.

"I love you," he answered back.

The familiar opening bars of "Unforgettable" began to play and Rhett slid his hands around Cole's shoulders, the ownership papers for the vineyard pressed tight between their chests.

"Dance with me," Rhett said.

Cole nodded, stealing one more kiss before looping his arms around Rhett's waist.

"For the rest of my life."

Epilogue
RHETT

When Rhett envisioned getting married at the Mallory Vineyard, he never imagined marrying a Mallory at the Mallory Vineyard. June twelfth was their unofficial first anniversary, the date they'd told people their first date took place. No one knew the truth.

The origins of their relationship were something they'd decided to keep to themselves, even though the ruse had long ago crossed the line from pretend to real. Rhett enjoyed having secrets with Cole. Little truths that belonged only to them made Rhett feel special and only added to the depths of his feelings for Cole.

Rhett straightened his tie, then slid into his jacket. Buttoning it quickly, he examined himself in the mirror. Sometimes he wondered what Cole saw in him. Rhett smiled at his reflection. It didn't really matter, he supposed. Rhett felt like Cole had been the first person to really see him, to see the man below the bookish surface and to embrace him for who he was. The way Cole looked at him sometimes still took Rhett's breath away. He couldn't begin to fathom how he'd gotten so lucky.

"There's the handsome groom," Penny said, appearing out of nowhere, Tyson perched on her hip in his tiny suit, flapping his chubby arms. "You almost ready?"

Rhett nodded and Penny smiled at him. "I'll send him in."

"There he is. The future Mr. Mallory."

Rhett turned and grinned at Cole taking in the sight of him all at once, then bit by bit, committing the sight of him to memory. "Mallory-Kingston," Rhett corrected.

"Are you ready, babe?"

Cole was devastatingly handsome in his black suit and his green tie, the same color as Lucy's foliage. It also happened to bring out the sage color in his eyes. He held his hand out for Rhett, like a question waiting for an answer.

Rhett took his hand. "Is this real?" he breathed as Cole tugged him close and brushed his lips against Rhett's. Their last kiss as fiancés.

"This is real, Rhett." Cole twined their fingers together and they walked down the stairs and out into the vineyard and down the aisle toward their guests. Penny stood front and center, a book open in front of her, ready to be the one to marry them and together they walked toward their family, their friends, and their future.

Rhett stood in front of them all and grabbed his dream with both hands. There were moments in the early days of their relationship when Rhett had felt as if he'd finally found everything he wanted, but he was terrified that for Cole it would never be as real as it was for him.

Penny pronounced them husband and husband, and Cole leaned in, his lips claiming Rhett's, his arms wrapping around him, pulling him close, tucking their bodies together, washing the last of Rhett's doubts away.

Cole pressed his lips near Rhett's ear. "This is real. You are the most real thing in my life, Mr. Mallory-Kingston."

Rhett returned Cole's sentiment with a kiss that had their family and friends clapping and cheering, but nothing could drown out Rhett's pulse, frantic in his ears, roaring with desperation to be alone with his husband.

Rhett laughed as Cole, his husband, kissed him for the

hundredth time that night. "You're going to wear my lips out before we even get to the honeymoon." Rhett let himself melt against Cole's side. "Which you still haven't told me where you're taking me."

"It's not a surprise if I tell you."

"You're no fun at all, Mr. Mallory."

"Mallory-Kingston. I happen to love the way my husband's name sounds next to mine."

"If you two get any more nauseating, people will start puking, they'll blame the wine, the entire vineyard will go bankrupt, your future will be ruined." Ryan exclaimed, his cheeks a lovely rosy pink color to match the wine that he'd clearly had enough of.

"Then we better just take off." Cole wrapped his arm around Rhett's waist and pretended to run away with him.

"Where's your date?" Rhett asked his brother, who shrugged a shoulder.

"Around. I think." Ryan seemed a little confused, but then shook it off. "I wanted to say goodnight to you guys." Ryan wrapped his arms around Rhett and hugged him tight. He whispered in Rhett's ear, his voice tight, "Mom would have loved this."

When Ryan pulled away, he looked at Rhett with glassy eyes, then nodded. He gave Cole a quick hug, then disappeared, maybe in search of his date.

"Can we get out of here soon?" Rhett asked, eager to be alone with his husband.

"Soon. There's one more person I need to talk to." Cole tugged Rhett over to Kristen, who had given birth scant weeks before the wedding. Her original due date, in typical Kristen fashion, had landed on Rhett and Cole's wedding date. Their niece, however, had other plans.

Kristen smiled at them as they approached, tiny Kate bundled in her arms. "Rhett, did you know that the girls are still talking about the baby shower you threw me?"

Rhett leaned in and kissed Kristen on the cheek, then glanced at his sleeping niece. "I bet they are. My evil plan was for it to be so grand that they'd all want to have babies just so I could plan baby showers for them."

Cole took baby Kate in his arms and Rhett's heart let out a happy sigh.

"Oh gross, you can't look at my brother like that when I'm right here." Kristen moaned, reaching for a bottle of water. "That's practically obscene. When are you leaving for your honeymoon?"

"Soon, actually." Cole handed Kate back to her mother. "Did I ever thank you, Kristen, for what you did for us?" Cole linked his hand with Rhett's and held it tight. "You gave us our dream." After Kristen's grand display at New Year's, which had impressed everyone except for their grandparents, Kristen and Cole's relationship had improved slightly, and her relationship with Rhett had done a complete one-eighty. Cole only pretended to hate that Rhett and Kristen were friends.

"Oh, my God." Kristen rolled her eyes. "Do not get all goopy and sappy on me. Save it for the husband."

"Oh, don't worry, I will," Cole said suggestively.

"Oh gross, Cole." Kristen made a face and Cole laughed, tugging Rhett away from the party.

"Is it time to leave for our honeymoon now?" Rhett asked. The honeymoon location was top secret and he hated being in the dark, but Cole had refused to divulge anything.

"Not yet, but it is time to be alone with my husband," Cole practically growled.

"Oh, thank God," Rhett exhaled as Cole stopped in a secluded section of the vineyard. They were bathed in the glow of a million twinkle lights and could hear the music from the reception softly playing.

Cole cupped Rhett's cheek and kissed him, his lips gentle and delicate. "Mr. Mallory-Kingston, will you dance with me?"

"For the rest of my life."

They danced in the vineyard under a galaxy of lights, humming bars from "Unforgettable." They danced pressed tight against the other, enjoying the quiet intimacy of the moment, until it built into something far more urgent and they went home to be truly alone.

※

Hours later, a very tired Rhett leaned against Cole in a crowded airport.

"Will you tell me now?" Rhett pleaded.

Cole laughed and kissed Rhett's cheek. "California to New York to France, to drink Bordeaux in Bordeaux."

An impossibility. A figment of his imagination. A future he never thought possible. "You're too good to be true," Rhett said, angling for a kiss.

"You're a dream come true."

"You're sappy."

"Of course I am. I'm in love with you."

Rhett smiled and kissed his husband in the middle of the crowded airport. He pulled away when a voice overheard announced their flight was boarding.

Once in the air, Rhett pulled out his e-reader and looked at Cole, who still hadn't started a movie.

"Aren't you going to watch something?" Rhett asked, turning it on.

Cole snuggled closer and tapped the screen of the e-reader. "Why don't you tell me more about this flirty dragon?"

Rhett's cheeks flushed. "Here?" Rhett glanced around the cabin, but no one seemed to be paying them any attention.

"Yes, here. I want my husband to read to me about flirty dragons and whatever else is in that book of his."

Rhett leaned over and kissed Cole. "I love being your husband."

"My very real husband. Now, please, I'm dying to know about the dragon."

Rhett chuckled. "I finished those books weeks ago."

"What are you reading now? Read that to me instead."

"Well, it's about this omega named Percy."

"Wait, what's an omega?"

"It may take a while to explain," Rhett warned with a smile.

"We have the rest of our lives." Cole captured Rhett's hand and brought it to his lips, brushing a kiss across the knuckles. "Read to me."

"Always," Rhett promised.

Acknowledgments

Kate here! E.M. is sound asleep in Canada and I've just finished edits which mean the acknowledgements page is ALL MINE.

maniacal laughter

E.M. came up with a crazy idea for an omegaverse story that we somehow turned into a fake relationship story for Rhett and Cole. We wrote this book STUPID fast. Unbelievably fast. If you want to know how fast, send one of us a message.

Anyway, this book wouldn't exist were it not for Melinda James Rueter, who is the best alphabeta on the planet. She lurked in our shared doc and read as we wrote so we could get it completed before our own self-imposed deadline.

Thank you to SJ Himes for being glorious and letting us talk about Eroch. If anyone was curious, all the books Rhett reads in Future Fake Husband are Sheena's. Eroch is from The Beacon Hill Sorcerer's Series and Percy is from Bred For Love, an mpreg series under the name Revella Hawthorne.

Brittany and Lisa, our brats...thank you for being the kind of readers we love to write for.

MUCH thanks to our cover artist Samantha (www.amaidesigns.com) for making sense of my vague color requests and always coming through with the most amazing covers.

Jordan Buchanan for being a great editor and leaving us the best comments.

And last but never least, if you're reading this, thank YOU. E.M. and I write because we want to make people happy and if you're here, we hope you're happy and that you enjoyed reading about Rhett and Cole's very real relationship as much as we enjoyed writing it.

About Kate Hawthorne

Born and raised in Southern California, Kate Hawthorne woke up one day and realized she had stories worth sharing. Now existing on a steady diet of wine and coffee, Kate writes stories about complicated men in love that are sometimes dirty, but always sweet. She enjoys crafting hard-fought and well deserved happy endings with just the right amount of angst and kink.

From estate sale shopping to shoe worship, there's something in at least one of her books that'll tickle your fancy. Visit her website at www.katehawthornebooks.com

Also by Kate Hawthorne

The Lonely Hearts Stories

His Kind of Love

The Colors Between Us

Love Comes After

Until You Say Otherwise

Giving Consent

Worth the Switch - a prequel

Worth the Risk

Worth the Wait

With E.M. Denning

Irreplaceable

About E.M. Denning

E. M. Denning is a married mom of three and a writer from British Columbia. Author of endearing filth and schmoopy sex, also addicted to books and coffee. She writes romance for the 18+ crowd.

Follow her on Facebook
Subscribe to her newsletter
Join her Facebook group Denning's Darlings

Also by E.M. Denning

The Desires Series
What He Needs

What He Craves

What He Hides

What He Fears

Upstate Education Series
Half as Much

With Kate Hawthorne
Irreplaceable

Future Fake Husband

—

All For Him

Boomerang

Revenge

Little Love on the Prairie

Measure For Measure

The Studio Collection
Alpha Tango

At The Barre

Jazz Hands

Break

The Forbidden Dance

Printed in Poland
by Amazon Fulfillment
Poland Sp. z o.o., Wrocław